THE AUTOBIOGRAPHY
of
MARY MAGDELENE

THE AUTOBIOGRAPHY
of
MARY MAGDELENE
A Novel

P. C. NAIR

THE AUTOBIOGRAPHY OF MARY MAGDELENE
A NOVEL

iUniverse books may be ordered through booksellers or by contacting:

iUniverse
1663 Liberty Drive
Bloomington, IN 47403
www.iuniverse.com
1-800-Authors (1-800-288-4677)

Because of the dynamic nature of the Internet, any web addresses or links contained in this book may have changed since publication and may no longer be valid. The views expressed in this work are solely those of the author and do not necessarily reflect the views of the publisher, and the publisher hereby disclaims any responsibility for them.

Any people depicted in stock imagery provided by Thinkstock are models, and such images are being used for illustrative purposes only.
Certain stock imagery © Thinkstock.

ISBN: 978-1-5320-2572-3 (sc)
ISBN: 978-1-5320-2573-0 (hc)
ISBN: 978-1-5320-2571-6 (e)

Library of Congress Control Number: 2017910976

Print information available on the last page.

iUniverse rev. date: 08/25/2017

To
Rajam, Indu, jeff, Ravi, and sofia

AUTHOR'S FORWARD.

This novel, An Autobiography of Mary Magdalene is about the life and times of Mary, the Biblical Character. It is written in the first person. One group of Christian theologians regard Mary as a sinner, and she attains salvation through Jesus. Another group thought of her as a devout follower of Jesus among Jewish women of that time period. Whatever the truth, even after 2000 years, the world has not forgotten her. They consider her as a savant and still worship.

My intention in this novel is to present Mary as a true follower of Christ who attained salvation through him. Here I also tried to give importance to Mary's significant contribution to the building up of early Christian church. It is indeed believed that Jesus respected Mary for her deep knowledge of God's Kingdom, and for her devotion to his ministry. Many of the incidents narrated in my novel are from the Gospels. Others also have historical basis. There are certain events not in the Gospels. For example the destruction of Jerusalem by the Romans. But it is vividly explained by the historian Josephus. Let me also mention briefly about the emotional bond between Mary and Jesus alluded to in my novel. Jesus was unmarried, and to all accounts a very handsome man. He was also a very charismatic person. Mary was an unmarried young woman (with an inquiring mind) who frequently travelled with him. Under the circumstance, there is nothing unusual to develop a friendly, personal relationship between them. Specifically, we must remember they were part of a group, who were going together to spread Gospels. So there could be attachment between a master and a pupil, or a leader and a follower.

I believe there is nothing uncommon in this view as I depicted. More over scholars have indicated that Jewish people of that time often greeted each other by embracing and sometimes kissing (even between men and women). After all, many do so even today. Jesus had genuine affection and respect for Mary's unique personality.

In short, I have depicted Mary as a woman, born and and bought up in a Jewish family in Jewish tradition who undertakes a pilgrimage, as a follower of Christ, and attains salvation through him. For generations, Mary who rarely appears in the Bible and her contribution to early church have been the subject of study by scholars. What is the basis of this? I believe it is because of her significant contribution in defining humanity, that is, in shaping the lives and thoughts of generations of people. For ages our forefathers have inquired about the meaning of humanity. The present generation also has to learn many things about this subject. In a sense, the story of Mary, this blessed woman, is a story about ourselves. I hope it will be received as such by the readers.

I also wish to acknowledge here my deep sense of gratitude to Ms. Margaret George whose novel Mary called Magdalene, has been a source of inspiration for me in writing this book.

CHAPTER 1

I was born into a Jewish family in Magdala, a small town on the western bank of the Sea of Galilee. My memories of my father and mother are very vague. When I was four years old, first my father and then my mother, a few months later, died of smallpox. My mother's younger sister, Ruth, brought me up.

Our home was in the valley of a small hill in the northern section of Magdala. It was decorated according to the Jewish tradition. Hanging on the doorpost was a mezuzah, a decorative container with a parchment on which words from the Torah, our sacred text, were inscribed. This old tradition of our people reminded us to live by God's commandments every time we entered or left our home.

Aunt Ruth lived her life according to strict Jewish tradition and beliefs. Since one of our beliefs was that it was our duty to feed helpless people as much as we could, Aunt Ruth always donated bread and butter to the needy families in our village. This gift was much appreciated by the townspeople of Magdala. They were poor, and they earned their livelihood mostly by fishing in the sea and selling the catch in nearby towns. But when there was high wind and rain, they couldn't sail their small boats into the sea, and they ended up going hungry if they had no catch to sell. As ours was a relatively wealthy family, my aunt Ruth didn't have any difficulty donating the necessary food.

Aunt Ruth believed that human beings are created in the image of God and that we all have a responsibility to take care of fellow human beings in need. And according to the laws of the Torah, providing for orphans was a great act of kindness, a practice called Beit Yetomim. So she loved to provide food, clothing, and shelter to children whose parents had died. She also visited the sick and infirm in our neighborhood.

Since Aunt Ruth gave great importance to religious rituals and beliefs, she prayed three times daily: morning, afternoon, and evening. She visited the synagogue every day too. She often took me to the morning service, *shacharit*, where she enthusiastically explained to me the meaning of every ritual in the worship.

The morning service always began with a set of introductory prayers and the singing of hymns. These set the mood and tone of the worship. The service lasted until ten o'clock in the morning.

Aunt Ruth then would attend the afternoon service, *minchah*, and the evening service, *ma'ariv*. She also attended *keriat haforah*, the weekly reading of the Torah. It was customary for our community to read it four times a week.

***

When Aunt Ruth wasn't at home, I usually spent my time playing with kids in the neighborhood or playing the organ, which I liked. When I was six years old, Aunt Ruth enrolled me in the school that was part of our synagogue.

My teacher, Rabbi Alphais, was an elderly gentleman with a flowing white beard and a smiling face who always wore a *kepah* of Torah.

Aunt Ruth didn't have any children of her own; her own husband had passed away soon after their marriage. Afterward, and directly due to this misfortune, she didn't possess much mental strength. It's no wonder she became deeply religious.

***

The most important thing Rabbi Alphais wanted me and the other students to have was reverence for God; we were always to obey God's laws and be obligated to him. Since this principle was a basic tenet of Jewish belief and identity, we accepted his instruction without hesitation.

In a calm but stern voice, Rabbi Alphais would start his teaching each day by giving thanks to God, our Savior: "Oh Lord, you are our only

God. May those who love you be secure. May there be peace within your walls." Then he would explain who God is and what he does. After this, Rabbi Alphais told us about the relationship between God and humanity.

I found out that our people believe that as time passes, God grows. So each person must discover, understand, and relate to God in his or her own way, out of his or her own life experience.

At first, the topics were very hard for us children to understand. However, Rabbi Alphais slowly explained them using parables children could easily understand. So, in due course, we students were able to understand the central meaning of these tenets.

But I remained skeptical about one thing the rabbi taught us. I found out that throughout Jewish history, God had always been referred to as a "Him" and not a "Her." I began to wonder why, and after I grew up somewhat, I asked my classmates about it. They said any suggestion that God might have female characteristics had been strongly rejected from the very beginnings of Judaism. They told me this was done to distinguish it from the nations and tribes at the time that worshipped several goddesses. I wasn't quite sure then, and now, that this explanation is satisfactory, for God is for everybody, regardless of a person's gender.

Rabbi Alphais always concluded his instruction by singing a song of prayer to God:

I will sing song for Yahweh.
He is our Lord.
My strength, my songs
Are Yahweh.
He was my Savior!
He is my God; I will praise thee!
Then we children would repeat this prayer after our teacher.

***

During my childhood, we celebrated many auspicious days. We had religious holidays, like Rosh Hashanah, Yom Kippur, and Passover, and social festivities, like Purim and Sukkot. I always liked to help Aunt Ruth to set up items for our rituals on the holidays, and we celebrated them together with joy.

Rosh Hashanah was a joyous occasion for children and adults alike.

It's the Jewish New Year, and it falls either in September or early October. We greeted the new year with serious introspection, self-evaluation, and prayer. We believed we could shape the future by assessing the successes and failures of the past.

On Rosh Hashanah, we prayed for good fortune, and we approached those days with due reverence. The new year begins with ten days of repentance, culminating in Yom Kippur, the Day of Atonement. On atonement day, we repented for the mistakes and transgressions we committed in the previous year, and we sought forgiveness from God. As is the custom, we also fasted on this day.

During Passover, we told the story of the slaves' exodus from Egypt with words, songs, and special foods. The Hebrew slaves had fled Egypt with such haste that the bread they made didn't have time to rise. So they ate unleavened bread thereafter. That's the reason we ate only flat bread during Passover and why food is central to the observance of Passover.

At Passover, we used special utensils to prepare the unleavened bread and other items to eat. Rabbinic sages prohibited our use of certain grains—wheat, barley, rye, and oat—presumably because leavened bread could be made from them.

Although many foods are excluded when preparing meals, there is a festive ritual meal called the Seder. The foods served on the Seder plate symbolically tell the story of Passover. Roasted egg, a green vegetable that was usually celery or parsley (*karpas*), bitter herbs (*maror*), a mixture of chopped meats, and nuts are the main items. The roasted egg symbolizes the wholeness and continuity of life. Karpas represents springtime and renewal. Maror, which is mostly horseradish, reminds everyone of the bitterness our people felt when they were slaves in Egypt.

During Passover, we used *Haggadah,* a book that recounts the events of the Exodus. It outlines the rituals that are to be performed during the course of the Seder meal and also contains psalms and other songs of praise to God for the many miracles he did while bringing Jewish people out of Egypt.

Passover got its name this way: At first, the Pharaoh, who was the king of Egypt, denied permission for Moses and his followers to leave his country. The king worried that if they were allowed to leave, there would be a shortage of slaves necessary to support the Egyptian economy. Due to

Even before Aunt Ruth's death, Sabed moved in to stay with us. He was older than me by three years. I found him always pleasant, with a constant smile on his face.

Sabed was also very efficient; he had an unusual knack for understanding things quickly. I liked him and came to regard him as my older brother. In turn, he treated me like a sister. Though my aunt had put Sabed in charge of conducting the daily business, I remained the owner. He never forgot that I was the important member in the family, and he always treated me that way.

For the family business, we had a large warehouse on the beach, as we needed storage space. When we lent silver coins to the fishermen, we collected jars of dried fish from them as surety. When they gave us back the money, we returned those jars to them.

I was nearing twenty years of age and had come to learn more about our business as time passed. One day, Sabed and I were sitting in a room in the warehouse, going over some accounts. An elderly man came into the room and stood there politely. I immediately recognized him as Nathan, a man who had worked for Aunt Ruth for several years. From the look on his face, it was clear that he had something important to tell us.

When I inquired as to what was on his mind, Nathan told us a heartbreaking story. "Harold Antipas is our king. He rules Judea under the authority of the Roman emperor. Since he shows his allegiance and gives support to the Roman authorities, the people in our land who long for freedom and liberty hate him. There are even people living among us who took an oath to annihilate him and the Roman soldiers if they ever get an opportunity. These individuals operate as a secret society, called "Sikri."

Although Nathan himself didn't have any interest in subversive activities, he gave his only son permission to do whatever he thought was just and right, and he told us his son belonged to that society.

Just a few months before, Sikri ambushed and killed a Roman soldier. The Romans conducted a widespread search for the killers. The only one they managed to capture was Nathan's son. Without an inquiry of any sort, they beheaded the young man, thrust his head on a spear, and displayed it for several days in the main junction of our village for all to see.

Nathan told us that his son's wife went mad upon seeing this gruesome sight, and he no longer knew where she was. In her absence, he had begun caring for his son's daughter, Alka. But he had become sick and infirm, and he was no longer able to continue caring for her. He also informed me his own wife had passed away recently.

In a voice that cracked with anguish, Nathan asked if I could provide a refuge for Alka. Since Jews believe that adopting orphans and caring for them is a sacred duty, I adopted this child without any hesitation. Sabed liked my decision.

The very next day, Nathan brought Alka to us. I liked the young girl from the moment I saw her. She was ten years younger than I.

Always genial, Alka was intent on doing whatever she could to make me happy. I felt I should bring her up with due diligence—and warmth.

In time, we became like sisters.

***

I often visited villages around Galilee to participate in Jewish faith festivals. I would go to them with Sabed and Alka, and we always were careful to return home before dark. While returning from one such festival, I saw a heartbreaking scene in our town's main junction.

As I relate this story, please be aware that I had only a vague knowledge at the time of the social and political conditions prevalent in Galilee and Judea. But I did know the Roman emperor, Tiberius, was our ruler, and I often spied Roman soldiers roaming around in our village.

That particular evening, two native Jews were traveling in front of our group. One was on a donkey; the other, on foot. When the Jews reached the main junction of several paths, one of a group of Roman soldiers standing there asked the man on the donkey to dismount.

The elderly traveler refused. The man on foot—perhaps the man's son—said something in an angry tone to the soldier. Without delay, the soldier began to thrash both men with his whip.

Ribbons of blood soon oozed out of the younger man's face and bare chest. Overcome with fear, the elderly man got down from his donkey. In a pleading voice, he promised the soldier he would walk the rest of the distance if he would stop striking them. Only then did the soldier cease.

This tragic event would not leave my mind, and from that moment on, I viewed Roman soldiers with hate and distrust.

On occasion, I saw these soldiers standing on our beach, looking east and saying something in their language. Later I found out from Sabed that they worshipped the sun, so what I was observing was their morning worship.

***

During Sukkot, it was a divine ritual for Jews to visit the temple Solomon had built in Jerusalem. The first temple he built had been destroyed by the neighboring hostile tribes. Later it was rebuilt—and destroyed again. Our Babylonian forefathers had constructed the last one around five hundred years before. It was of great importance to them, and a pilgrimage to the temple was a must for every Jew.

When I reminded Sabed of this, he indicated his desire to go on a pilgrimage to the temple with me. Three or four neighboring families expressed interest in coming along with us. Since Sabed and I had known all of them for a long time, I agreed, thinking they would help us in our journey, as we needed to pitch tents and prepare food while traveling.

It took us three days to travel on donkeys from our village to Jerusalem, as the terrain was rough. We set out on the pilgrimage on the morning of the appointed day. We traveled on the backs of five donkeys, bringing our own food and bedding with us.

When the sun became extremely hot, we rested in the shade of fig trees for a while. The children of our neighbors didn't seem tired though; they shouted excitedly and clamored loudly to see the temple. After a while, we continued on our journey, even though we didn't feel rested.

On the third day at sunset, our party reached the western ridge of a small hill overlooking the holy city of Jerusalem. We all got down from the donkeys and looked down at the city below us with awe and wonder.

How can I even describe the sight we saw?

Inside the four walls of the city, the land was flat. Streets paved with red cobblestones glowed under the red rays of the sun. The golden temple was in the far eastern portion of the walled city, and around the temple were many white marble palaces.

I spied numerous pilgrims of all ages from the other villages of Israel, carrying offerings to the temple—either sacks of barley on their backs or baskets full of grapes or apples in their arms. It was the custom to offer God the first cut of our harvest.

The air itself resounded with the sounds of bugles, guitars, and various other musical instruments. Everybody was singing praise to the Lord.

We moved closer to the city and erected a large tent. That first night, Sabed, Alka, and I stayed in the tent with the families who had come with us from Magdala. It was difficult for me to sleep amid the constant noise made by the other pilgrims.

Although we were short of sleep and tired, the next morning our group set out to see the temple right away. Our desire to see it—even to come closer to it—was intense.

We discovered that the main street that led in the direction of the temple ended in the vicinity of a huge Roman fortress, Antoine. There, rows of soldiers stood guard on its steps with spears in their hands.

From that spot, we had to walk half a mile through a narrow street to reach the eastern gate of the temple. Our party reached the temple before the sun was high in the sky.

The temple, built with gold panes and white marble, glittered in the early-morning light. Its golden domes stood above the dark-green leaves of the surrounding cypress trees. I found the place marvelous. However, something else I saw there made me sad: in front of the eastern gate of the temple, which was kept open, sat a long row of beggars and sick people.

To keep law and order as the pilgrims moved forward, a few soldiers were posted at both sides of the gate. As we approached the wide-open space around the temple, it soon filled with all kinds of curious-looking people who talked in languages I didn't recognize and dressed in different-colored clothes. There were merchants trying to sell sacrificial lambs and caged birds, and traders from Persia offered beautiful gold brocade. There were moneychangers of all kinds too. The site was like a busy marketplace.

Rows of priests dressed in red gowns with little blue stars stitched onto them stood at both sides of the front door to the temple. Near them, well-dressed children sang hymns and played guitars and flutes. A sign hanging above the main gate to the temple read, "No admittance for non-Jews." The punishment for those who violated this rule? Hanging.

I thought that in the inner temple there must be something sacred: the tablet containing the Ten Commandments, a portion of Noah's ark, or King Aaron's rod. I thought that must be why it was forbidden to go in. But when we found out it was empty and inquired as to why no sacred relics were within, a priest replied that such things had been destroyed in the Babylonians' attack after the reign of King Solomon.

It was disappointing to me that all those inflexible laws about entering the temple involved worship at an empty place. While the temple was magnificent in its physical appearance, I thought it lacked purity in the spiritual sense. Inside, I didn't see any significant symbols of the Jewish faith, like a menorah—a seven-branched candelabrum—a symbol of the nation of Israel and our mission to be "a light into other nations." Early the next morning, disappointed, we returned home with haste.

***

After our return to Magdala, I started a new routine: visiting the beach every evening. I found I needed to get away from all my chores for at least a few hours each day.

It was my practice to help Sabed daily with the accounts and purchases for our business. It was also my duty to listen to the grievances of employees and to find appropriate solutions for them. Although these were necessary tasks, I got bored with them. Plus, I wanted to be alone. That's why I liked my evening walk to the beach.

I always headed there through the center of the town, where there was a pathway laid with blue cobblestones leading up to the most beautiful part of the beach. To the left of the path, once it reached the beach, were two rock formations visible above the water. These were round, but had two large holes on top, each one large enough for a person to sit in comfortably. I always liked to settle into one of them and take off my sandals and put them in my small bag. Then I would sit there watching the gentle waves wash ashore.

It was indeed an exhilarating experience to dangle my feet in the blue water as I gazed at the sunset. Sometimes, on hot days, there was an additional blessing in the form of a mild sea wind.

On one of my daily visits to the beach, I met Abigail. That evening, the sea was slightly tumultuous. While I was returning from the rocks to the beach itself—which was less than two hundred feet away from my usual hiding place—a big wave came roaring over me. I was terrified it would take me into its fold as it receded. I lay in the water trembling with fear, not knowing what to do.

A woman who was watching the event unfold came rushing toward me. She held me up with both her hands and placed me back on the top of the rock. She was strong. We both stayed there for a few minutes, waiting for the waves to subside. When we felt the danger was over, we scurried to the beach.

When we reached safety, the woman who had risked her own life to save mine looked at me intently for a few seconds. She then cautioned, "Do not come here alone. No one can say when the sea gets violent."

I didn't say anything in reply, but I presented her with a short smile tinged with sincere thanks.

She then said her name was Abigail and that she lived in Magdala too. Also, as a matter of pleasantry, she expressed her hope that we should meet again before she departed.

After this unexpected encounter, Abi and I started to meet on the same rock almost every day. I told her my name and said I also lived in Magdala.

Eventually Abi and I became friends.

***

Abi's father, a prosperous merchant, came from Greece. Her mother was Jewish.

Abi was only three or four years older than me. She was married but told me that their relationship wasn't in the best shape. Her husband, also a Greek, was a partner in her father's business. Through this partnership, Abi's husband had made an immense fortune for himself.

Abi told me their business made money buying huge quantities of dried fish from local businessmen and then selling them in countries like Syria and Greece. Abi's husband was a generous man, and he was very fond of her. He always showered her with many expensive gifts. However, he somehow wasn't able to give her what a woman desires most from her husband: nearness and emotional attachment to her. Since her husband was always traveling on business, it was rare for him to sleep in their house.

Abi was a model of extreme Greek beauty. She had attractive eyes, although I felt they were a bit sad. She also had a radiant smile, neatly kept fingers, and a shapely body. These features added to her innate charm.

One day, Abi invited me and two other girls from our neighborhood to her house for dinner. We spent the evening merrily dancing and singing.

I discovered that evening that Abi could imitate the sounds of both a parrot and a dove. She gave us a presentation of this in the form of a brief conversation between the two birds. It was very entertaining indeed.

As the time we spent together was a Sabbath day, the parents of the other children arrived to take them home. Since my house was very near Abi's, and I had complete freedom, I had accepted her invitation to stay overnight. Truly, I didn't give it much thought.

We went to bed early. Abi made up a bed for me in one room. Before she left to sleep in hers, she asked me to give the caged parrot in my room some milk and a parcel of rice as feed in the morning. I agreed. I was tired, and soon I slept.

In the middle of the night, I heard someone slowly opening the door. A shadow crept toward me. Through the faint moonlight shining in from the open window, I could see that it was Abi. She came near me and said we could go into the garden and spend some time together there.

I arose and proceeded with her to the beautiful garden, enveloped in the light of the full moon. We sat silently for a while on a small couch under the middle of the arbor, holding each other's hands.

I stared at the arbor, adorned as it was by grapevines and many flowers. I noticed gold swans swimming around in the pond in front of the arbor. One male swan was trying to appease a female swan so that he might tryst with her. The full moon began to rise all the way up into the wide sky. I do not remember how long we sat there.

It happened suddenly. Abi put her right hand over my shoulder and brought her face closer to mine. Her breathing became intense. Blood gushed through my veins, and I could not control myself. Embracing her, I kissed her over and over again.

"Kli! Kli!" The parrot's voice woke me up.

By this time, the sun's rays had spread through the room, pushing away the light of the moon.

CHAPTER 3

Months and then years passed, sometimes slowly—and at other times hastily. All the girls who had studied with me in the school attached to the synagogue married and had children. But I was still unmarried.

I hadn't made a decision as to whether marriage was for me. Truth was, up until then, I hadn't been all that interested in it. Moreover, the girls in my class still had parents to take care of their affairs. Cruel fate had denied me that. So if I wanted to marry, it would be up to me to find myself a suitable groom.

In those days, singleness was a shameful state; it wasn't customary. I desired what everybody else wanted: blessings from God and a model life, complete with family, wealth, health, and a house of one's own. Who would not wish to have those?

Yet at the same time, I liked my independence. I already had whatever one could achieve by marriage. I had wealth and a home of my own. All I was lacking was a family with a husband and children who played outside.

But what was the price I should give for them? If I married, I would be obligated to fulfill the needs of my husband and children every day and night. The liberty I had enjoyed so far would be lost. At a practical level, I would become like a slave. Was I ready for that?

The Torah mentioned that orphans and single women were a burden to society. However, I had plenty of money to live comfortably, so I felt I was no burden. I also knew that women who came from Greece and Syria had more freedom than women from Magdala, as they didn't have to wear a head scarf once they were wed.

It was very difficult for me to find an answer to whether or not I wanted to seek a husband.

***

From the beginning, Jewish religious traditions were an integral part of my upbringing. Daily I recited all ten commandments. As I read each commandment, I bowed my head and sought mercy from Yahweh.

On the Day of Atonement, I would repent and pray fervently for forgiveness. If I committed any sin in the previous year, I would seek forgiveness from God.

Jewish tradition dictates that forgiveness can be sought only from God. However, for transgressions between people, forgiveness should first be sought and obtained from the people who were offended.

I believed in the Ten Commandments given to the children of Israel at Mount Sinai. The list begins with "Thou shalt have no other gods before me." The second says, "Thou shalt not make unto thee any graven image." Till I met Jesus, I believed in them.

I felt guilty when it came to the fourth commandment, which says, "Remember the Sabbath day by keeping it holy." I always remembered my tryst with Abigail on a Sabbath day.

The fifth one says, "Honor thy father and thy mother." This didn't apply to me.

The sixth says, "Thou shalt not kill." I didn't.

The seventh says, "Thou shalt not commit adultery." I wasn't quite sure about that commandment.

So I adhered to most commandments. However, I found some too restrictive for my taste.

I held strong views on other matters too. Regarding the creation of humanity in this universe, I believed that man and woman had equal importance. Because of this, I had difficulty understanding God's edicts. In the holy book were references about God's commandments to Abraham, Moses, and Solomon, but apparently God had spoken only rarely to women. One of those times was to announce to Mary that she would have a baby boy.

I tried hard to believe that God didn't have such a discriminatory approach. Then I remembered Eve, Sarah, and Hannah. God had told

Eve that he would make childbearing difficult and birth painful. In the case of Sarah and Hannah, he had ordered that they would have sons, not daughters. The feeling that God through his commandments didn't treat woman as equal to man was always a source of discomfort for me. Later I found comfort and peace in realizing the supreme power of a female deity. More on that later.

***

Three years before, the Roman emperor, Augustus Caesar, had passed away. He had ruled a vast empire for a very long time, and he had several queens. But he never had a son to succeed him, and so he had to adopt a son. A year after Augustus's death, the Romans declared him a god. I felt that they were humiliating the true God.

Caesar's adopted son, Tiberius, was the man who ascended to the throne. He didn't have any qualities required for an emperor. He was a coward, always suspicious of others.

To please Tiberius, King Antipas built a town about twenty miles from Magdala and named it Tiberias. It was a modern city built in the Greco-Roman architectural style. It had straight streets and a large stadium on its outskirts. Orthodox Jews never visited this town, as it wasn't under the control of Jewish religious authorities. The authorities viewed the town as a refuge for pagan worshippers, prostitutes, and gamblers. However, in due course, Tiberias gained a reputation as an important trading center. Expensive dresses from Greece and Egypt, sharp swords from Syria, and nuts and fruits from Persia became available there.

One festival season, Sabed and I decided to visit Tiberias. He was always interested in travel, as it afforded him an opportunity to see new sights.

As we made our way toward the center of the town, we passed a shrine dedicated to a pagan god. There was a white marble statue of Aesculapius, the Greek and Roman ideal of vigor and health. The huge statue was half-naked with its private part covered only by a loin cloth. A fountain in front of the statue spouted water about the god's feet. Around the fountain, throngs of people chanted hymns and danced. Everybody seemed to be imbued by a divine spirit.

Sabed and I stood there for a short while. We watched as the people around us prayed to the god that they could have some respite from all the ills that had befallen them. At that precise moment, I felt I was one of them.

My mind was always troubled. I didn't have any monetary woes, as I was reasonably wealthy. But because of my views on the status of women in society, which I didn't hide from others, I was seen as weird. In male-dominated social gatherings, I felt I was treated as an outcast. Managing a somewhat large business enterprise was also stressful.

We found the main marketplace of the town both busy and boisterous. There were all kinds of men—merchants, traders, and travelers—milling around the large town square. There also were women carrying baskets full of flowers and fruit, donkeys transporting travelers, and serious-looking men of the town walking hastily. We also saw shopkeepers standing in front of the shops and calling people's attention to their wares. The cleanliness and vibrancy of the place impressed me. There were no beggars there.

We planned to stay in Tiberias for three days. Sabed rented two rooms for us in a guesthouse. Until dusk on the first day, he and I wandered around the main square, watching various events. Then, when it turned dark, we returned to the guesthouse.

It was a small house with three rooms and was operated by an elderly couple that kept it very clean. They rented the two rooms available to us and stayed in the third room themselves. Though she was quite elderly, the matron of the house was very energetic and cared for us with both warmth and courtesy.

My room was rather small, but cozy; I didn't feel the cold from outside. I pulled the sheet over my face as I tried to fall sleep, but for a time, I simply couldn't. I lay there, curled up, trying to forget all I'd seen during the day: the white marble statue of the half-naked Aesculapius; the fountain spouting water around the god's feet; the people fervently praying in front of the pagan god.

I also prayed. *Oh God! Please forgive me for my trespasses!*

Everywhere, silence.

After a short while, I slept, but had frightening dreams.

I am traveling in the Sea of Galilee in a small boat, going through water near the shore. A clear blue sky is overhead. Seabirds fly above me, angling to devour fish.

The sea is calm.

My boat is going forward slowly. Suddenly, there is a lightning bolt and then a loud clap of thunder.

The sea is getting angry. I paddle my boat as fast as I can.

As if to swallow me up, a big wave comes roaring toward me. A waterspout comes after it that turns my boat upside down. All the water in the Sea of Galilee pulls my boat down, down, down.

Everywhere, darkness.

I swim.

I reach a small cave in an outcropping of rocks. I walk through an endless corridor. To save my life, I walk and walk.

Finally, I reach a beautiful garden. The darkness is gone! Up in the sky, a full moon is spreading its cool light all around.

I look around: I am in an arbor enveloped by grapevines. In front of the arbor is an artificial pond with swans playing merrily in it. One male swan is doing something in an attempt to woo a female swan into a tryst.

I look eagerly into the arbor. The small, decorated couch is not there.

I feel like crying, but the sound does not come out.

Where am I?

I opened my eyes and looked around. The room looked the same as it had when I went to sleep. Everything around me was in the same place.

But I could feel the cold from outside. I put on a woolen sweater before I went out onto the balcony.

I sat in the chair out there with a heavy heart and a burning sensation inside. Nothing was clear to me anymore.

Shortly, daylight broke out. I looked beyond the valley at a small hill in the distance and spied goats grazing there. Their shepherd was sitting on a low-lying branch, playing a guitar.

The swans playing in the artificial lake came back into my mind. They arrived in a form, like traces of white clouds. Then they became clearly etched in my mind.

I thought of the male swan. He wanted to be with the female. From their union there would be eggs; once those eggs hatched, small swans would be born. *This is a reproductive process that can be seen in every living* being, including human beings, I thought. *So can I justify before God the carnal union I had shared with Abi on the Sabbath, even if it was only in a dream?*

"No! No!" somebody shouted into my ears.

Who was saying that? There is no one near me! Perhaps—I am possessed? I have heard there are many in Magdala who are possessed by devils.

It was said that each devil had its own characteristics. The general belief was that if one devil entered into somebody, it would attract other devils with the same characteristics as the person it had entered.

Is this what is happening to me? I wondered.

***

Because of the dream and the unpleasant thoughts it evoked, I felt uneasy. So we cut short our visit by a day and headed for our homes in Magdala.

On the way back, when the sun was setting and spreading darkness around us, we had to cross a shallow stream. At first it seemed that this would be no problem, because the water was only knee-deep, and I was riding on a donkey. However, there were sharp stones and hidden holes beneath the water, making the passage treacherous. So we were going across, but moving forward very carefully.

Most of the time, I was looking down at the water, but at one point, I raised my head and looked to the bank on the other side of the stream. There I saw four or five people standing. I thought perhaps their faces were covered with black scarves, but as it was dark and hard to see, I wasn't quite sure.

Is danger lurking everywhere?

I grew anxious. The area we were in was desolate. I knew a few travelers were coming up behind us, but they were far back.

Sabed and I went forward, determined to face any situation. I was right: the faces were covered by black scarves. When we came near the group, a fellow—I guessed he was their leader—asked us to stop. Though Sabed is gentle by nature, when circumstances demand, he can be rude as well. "You mind your own business," he said curtly. "We are in a hurry to reach home!" He walked forward, and I stayed on my donkey.

The leader of the group gave a signal, and a person from the group jumped in front of Sabed with a sword.

While traveling outside Magdala, Sabed always carried a small iron rod for protection. He swiftly blocked the man's hand with this rod and then with his other hand reached over and lifted the scarf covering the face of the leader.

"Stop this nonsense! Don't I know you?" Sabed said with evident derision.

"Death to the people who collaborate with the enemy!" the leader cried out in response.

"Hanis, you know very well that I do not collaborate with the enemy. Be that as it may, come next month to the warehouse, and I will give you the usual contribution," Sabed said in an indifferent tone.

At once, I understood everything. These were members of the Sikri, those labeled by the Roman authorities as a terrorist group.

After the leader apologized several times for the inconvenience they had caused us, they disappeared into the darkness.

Later Sabed told me he had recognized Hanis by his voice.

***

Winter was over. The gusty wind that capsized fishermen's boats wouldn't come by again for quite some time.

But spring didn't usher in, although bands of birds now flew over the sea, back from wherever they had been hiding in search of prey. Even on such days, I used to see Abigail almost daily. We both derived pleasure in each other's presence.

Mostly, we met in her house. On occasion she would come to mine. At other times, we met at our meeting place among the rocks, on the beach.

Once Abi recited a Greek poem for me from one of the books she was reading. I could understand spoken Greek a bit, but I didn't know how to read or write it. Abi agreed to teach me to read that rich language, and in three or four months, I was able to read slowly so that I could understand books in Greek.

I bought some books, such as the *Iliad*, from a bookstore in town that secretly sold them, for the Magdala authorities had banned books written in foreign languages. I discovered that close contact with such valuable books widened my mind and strengthened my intellect.

I tried to gain nearness to God by reading sacred books as well.

***

One day I went to bed early. The next day was Yom Kippur, the Jews' day of atonement. As I lay in bed, the events of the past year went through my mind. I considered what I had to seek forgiveness for.

Ever since my return from Tiberias, I had been hearing different voices that gave instructions to me after calling out my name. These voices admonished me for my transgressions of the past.

"Mary," called out a low voice. It was one of the voices I had been hearing for some time. "Your servant is ready to listen," I answered in a humble but sleepy tone.

Abruptly, I forced myself awake. *After all, this is God talking to me,* I thought.

"Did you not commit sin during Sabbath?" the voice asked.

My heart trembled as the voice went on. God was referring to the tryst I had with Abi. "You do not know it yet, but you are possessed," the voice pronounced. Its echo lingered on in my ear.

After a short while, another voice spoke to me. This was one I had never heard before. "What you just heard is the voice of a false god. Do not obey it."

"Who are you?" I asked.

"I am Malarch," spoke the male voice.

"What do you want?" I asked fearfully.

"You should worship me as God. I give you all you need: health, wealth, beauty, and friends." Upon saying this, the voice laughed haughtily.

This time, I didn't say anything. What could I say?

"From the very beginning, the Israelites worshipped several gods. Why are you worshipping Yahweh only?" The voice now gave a roar in place of the laughter.

I kept silent.

"Can you worship only me?"

I stayed silent, and the male voice, apparently taking this as my consent, stopped talking. I lay there without moving for a time. The words of the earlier voice—"You are possessed"—kept ringing in my ears.

The next day, at Yom Kippur, I recited all my sins and prayed again for forgiveness.

Around this time, a possessed man created a sensational scene in Magdala. He came in a small boat into one of the wharfs in town. As soon as he landed, he ran into the town square. There he attempted to climb up the tower that graced the square. But the security officer there gave him a beating with his spear and drove him away.

Dancing weirdly and uttering obscure words, the man ran back to the center of the square. In a short time, several people gathered to see this unusual man and his antics. I wasn't interested in seeing him, so I told the others in our warehouse I didn't want to go with them.

However, when Sabed returned from viewing the man, I suddenly felt like I had to see him myself. Bad dream after bad dream, a constant headache, and depression—all of these had made me quite unsettled. I knew I might not be in the same state as that poor creature, but I had to go see a man who surely was possessed like me.

I arrived at the square just as the possessed man raised a clenched fist in the air. Then he bent down, and placing his hands on the ground, began walking like an animal. As he did so, foam began coming out of his mouth.

Suddenly he straightened up and addressed the folks who had assembled to watch him there. "Please have mercy on me! How did I come here? Is it from the demon that possessed me a long time ago?!"

"Who are you?" the town magistrate asked the man. The magistrate was among the people who had assembled at the square to see this spectacle. Keeping law and order was his primary duty.

"My name is Benjamin—" the man started, but he didn't have the strength to say the rest. He suddenly fell on the ground as foam gushed out of his mouth.

The magistrate quickly made arrangements to exorcise Benjamin, as all the people assembled there had concluded the man was indeed possessed by Satan. For exorcisms, the town relied on a renowned exorcist, Rabbi Gideon.

Gideon was sent for, and in a short while, he arrived. Benjamin, saying something in an alien language no one understood, was lying on the ground, groaning and moaning.

When Benjamin saw Gideon, he tried to get up, uttering, "Ha, you foolish old man, did you come to catch me?"

"In the name of Yahweh, I am asking you to come out of Benjamin, one of the sons of Abraham," Gideon said in a commanding tone.

"Who are you to order me about like this? Who gave you the authority for it? I am not going to obey you!" protested the demon in Benjamin in an adamant voice.

"I am asking you in the divine name of the Lord! Now leave this man alone!" Gideon ordered the demon with determination. "I am the Lord's servant, and I have power over *you*, who are the devil. You must leave this man."

At first, Benjamin's body shook violently. Then he fell to the ground and began rolling over. After saying something in a begging voice, he got up. One of the onlookers gave him some cold water to drink from a leather pouch.

After a short while, Benjamin's body stopped moving violently. He then covered his eyes with both hands and began to sob. It seemed to me, Gideon's effort to exorcise the demon out of Benjamin had succeeded.

Now that the immediate crisis was over, I wanted to know why and how the demon had gotten ahold of Benjamin. So I approached the rabbi quietly and inquired about the matter to him.

Rabbi Gideon explained it to me this way: "Benjamin didn't wish this. Because of ignorance, though, he committed a sin. This gave the demon an opportunity to get into him. We become possessed by committing sins. So we should be careful not to bring the wrath of God upon us by committing sins."

I stayed silent after this, and as I walked away, I wondered, *Will I also have Benjamin's fate?*

The possibility worried me.

***

I felt possessed again. It came in the form of an illusion.

This time, I was sitting alone in the warehouse. On the glass pane in the window across from me, I spotted blood flowing down. In the very next moment, it seemed the blood had started flowing up the pane.

I was confused, so I went to the pane and touched it. When I pulled my finger back, I looked, and there was no blood on my finger.

That evening I came home afraid of hearing Malarch's outrageous laughter. And when I went to bed that night, I could not sleep.

When I went for a walk to the beach or simply sat in the warehouse to work, feelings of guilt about the physical pleasure I had taken with Abi tormented me. I kept seeing the sight of swans in the pond on the Sabbath day. *What will be my escape?*

***

It was night.

I was in bed, trying to get some sleep.

"You are a sinner! You are not worshipping me."

Again, Malarch.

But now there was another devil threatening me often: Pazuzu, the god of death and destruction.

I wasn't happy with this life I was living. Clearly, it was becoming a burden to me.

I knew Sabed and Alka were asleep. They were like that: as soon as they hit the bed, they fell asleep. Because of this, I felt jealous of them sometimes.

So, knowing no one in my home would notice, I went out into the dim moonlight. It felt as if the sea were calling out to me, and I walked to it as if I were sleepwalking. My destination was one of the large lakes by the beach, which we called Harp, because it was shaped like the musical instrument. It was two miles long and half a mile or so wide. The place where it joined with the sea was a semicircle, and that was the place where the lake was the deepest. In that part of the lake were two wharfs for fishermen to anchor their boats.

I sat in one of the empty boats there. The sky was barren of stars, and silence was everywhere. The water in the lake began to swirl about. I looked down into it, and there I saw a reflection of the ugly face of Pazuzu, with its round red eyes, narrow forehead, thick lips, and tongue twisting out of an open mouth.

It seemed like this devil was playing hide-and-seek with me, appearing and disappearing in the waters of the lake.

I heard then a melody arising from lake, but for some reason, I didn't like its tune. I took a rope from the bag I had brought with me and tied my legs together at the ankles.

Praying to Yahweh, I jumped into the blue water. *Let my decomposing body be food for sea snakes or whales!*

I sank deep into the water—and I drowned.

Pazuzu must be roaring with delight!

CHAPTER 4

I regained consciousness to find Alka and Sabed beside me. I could see the dark shadow of extreme pain on their faces. With some shock, I realized I was in my own room—in my own bed! Placing my face on the pillow, I cried.

I do not remember how long I despaired like that. When I got up, I felt somewhat relieved though. The tears must have washed away some of my anguish.

I drank the fruit juice Alka held out for me, and slowly, the numbness in my head disappeared. I began to return to the reality around me.

"Do you feel a bit better now?" Sabed asked.

I didn't know what to say. Any attempt to smile was in vain. Because of the extreme hopelessness I'd felt in and about my life, I had jumped into the lake the previous night. That feeling was still a large part of me.

Because of my silence, Sabed stepped in to narrate briefly the events that had occurred after I made my jump. This wasn't a pleasant affair for any of us.

Apparently, when I had arrived at Harp, two fishermen had been anchoring their boats in a nearby wharf. They had returned home later than normal, with nets full from that day's catch. These men used to come to our warehouse on business, and at one time had been our customers. So one of them had recognized me and been surprised to see me alone at the wharf at night.

The moment I jumped into the lake, both men had jumped in after me. They found me, took me out of the water, and laid me on a plank on the beach. One of them stayed to watch over me, while the other hastened to my home to inform Sabed. Soon thereafter, Sabed and Alka arrived and brought me home.

This was the gist of what Sabed said. I heard what he said, but I remained silent.

Weeks went by with me not speaking to anyone.

***

Once Sabed visited some villages on the banks of the Jordan River on business. He stayed there for weeks. He was very happy to be able to spend time with his old friend and classmate, Jacob, whose family was in one of those villages.

Upon his return, Sabed told me the following things, which he had learned from the people he'd met through Jacob.

Compared to the shores of Galilee, Jordan's riverbed was more fertile. The people of that region were conservative in terms of religious matters. Because of the faulty administration in that region, most of the people were poor, illiterate, and sick.

One day a prophet by the name of John came among those thoroughly dispossessed people. Sabed had seen this man with the long beard and flowing hair for himself. Apparently, he was a man who didn't have any interest in comfortable living. He wore a gown made of animal skin and a worn pair of sandals. And his piercing eyes and commanding, high-pitched voice distinguished him from the rest of the country folks.

This prophet, John, told the village people that the arrival of the kingdom of God was imminent and that those who repented would attain salvation. Night and day he traveled through the villages to induce people to repent. As a sign of their repentance, John baptized them.

The practice of baptism had existed since ancient times. However, John gave it a new meaning. He washed people with water, in the Jordan River, as a sign of religious purification and devotion to God. It was an important step of obedience in a believer's life and an acknowledgement of salvation already accomplished.

This was, indeed, new information for me, and I found that John's prophecies gave me comfort. It was only natural for me to feel this way, due to the condition I was in. Always I felt depressed.

I spent most of my days from then on helping Sabed draw up a plan to increase the income from our business. Also, from time to time, I helped him adjust the accounting books.

Eventually, I resumed my routine of going to the beach for fun. I found I needed peace and happiness at that point, and my visits to the beach gave me a measure of that. However, even at this juncture in my life, sadness often disturbed me.

One morning, I woke up late with a slight headache. I opened my eyes, and the entire room where I was lying acquired an interesting blue color. Yet I knew that outside it was cold, and the sun's rays hadn't yet warmed the earth.

Suddenly, I saw a vase sitting on the small side table disappear. In its place appeared an old copy of the Torah. The pages were continually turning. I looked around, but there was nobody there who could be flipping through these pages. There was no wind sweeping into the room either.

I became very unsettled. I lay in the bed, because I was full of fear. For a short while, I slept.

A dream came, and I saw Pazuzu in it. I knew I had seen him somewhere before, and I frantically tried to remember where it had been. *Maybe in Tiberias?*

Yes, that was it. One of the storefront shops had exhibited the god's fearsome image. In a busy walkway littered with shops selling honey from Africa, and perfumes and dried fruits from Arabia, there had been a small, narrow shop. It was there that I had seen the gruesome image of Pazuzu. I wondered why the owner of that shop had kept that figure. Probably he thought it would ward off evil influences.

My attention quickly returned to the room before me. With shock, I realized that Malarch, who was much shorter in stature than Pazuzu, was lurking behind the latter. His face wasn't clearly visible to me, but he began roaring, as if to agree with whatever Pazuzu was saying.

Pazuzu addressed me thus: "Mary, are you still worshipping that false God? What will you get in return for doing that? Take that Torah off the table, and burn it."

Malarch roared at me, "Soon! Do as Pazuzu says."

In a low voice, I replied in a very humble tone, "I do not have the strength to do it. Yahweh is my God. Till I die, I will worship him only."

I listened to such talk patiently. I imagined these people felt some solace in finding a person who at least listened to their woes.

Alka began to call these weekly meetings a "union." When a union was over, we served bread and butter to the people. I entrusted that task to Sabed.

The information I gleaned from these unions inspired me to collect and study information regarding the sociopolitical conditions prevalent in Palestine at the time. I was particularly interested in learning the role played and the influence exerted by the Jewish priests in our society.

I came to understand, to a large extent, the economic status of the common people. I also understood—somewhat—the role current political factors were playing in shaping the lofty status of the Jewish priests in our society.

By understanding the times, I knew I could better help others understand Jesus's ministry in Galilee and the blessing it was conferring on my people. The following is what I knew and what I discovered.

During that time, Galilee and its adjoining province of Peria were ruled by a Jewish king: Antipas. He was the son of the great King Herod, the ruler who had rebuilt the temple in Jerusalem.[1]

However, Antipas didn't have any of the stellar qualities of his father, Herod. He was untrustworthy and selfish. He didn't have any interest in the welfare of his own people.

The administration in Judea lay in the hands of Antipas's elder brother, Archilas. Both ruled their fiefdom under the tutelage of the Romans. To the Grecian-Roman authorities, they showed immense allegiance.

People hated being under the rule of the cruel and selfish Archilas. After several years of protests by the people, the Roman emperor, Tiberius, removed him from power and bought Judea under direct Roman rule.

At that time, Pontius Pilate was the Roman procurator in Judea. He was hungry for power, and people called him "the magistrate." Although the emperor had appointed him to administer justice, Pilate was a cruel and deceitful man who didn't hesitate to do anything to achieve political gain for himself.

---

[1] In those days, Palestine included Judea, Samaria, Jerusalem, Galilee, Tyre, and many villages in the Jordan valley.

In Palestine, Roman authorities used prominent Jews as their tax collectors. For this purpose, they divided the country into small administrative districts. To each district, they appointed a prominent Jew who became responsible for collecting a fixed amount from villagers each year and handing it over to the Roman government. However, a tax collector could collect any amount he wished; the Roman procurator would not interfere. In many instances, the tax collectors exacted exorbitant amounts of money from the people to enrich themselves.

This method of tax collection proved a huge burden for the common people. They suffered immensely as a result, and they resented this method.

In the Jewish community were three distinct strata of people. The Pharisees were in the upper strata. They strictly obeyed the laws of Moses and other tenets added to them through the centuries. They were also interested in teaching these laws to others.

The Sadducees were the second strata. They were mostly priests, and they functioned in the upper echelons of society. They had great influence on the religious affairs of the people. It was the opinion of the Sadducees that the Israelites should live peacefully under the Roman authorities.

The sons of the soil belonged to the lowest strata. They were the majority of the people in our land, and they were mostly poor. Generally, they agreed with the Pharisees in political matters. And although they respected the Pharisees for their religious scholarship, they bitterly hated the tax collectors among them.

Although Jesus generally maintained a cordial relationship with all of these groups, his sympathies were with the sons of the soil who yearned for redemption. He got heavily involved with them—much more so than with the other two groups. He preached actively to them about the coming of the kingdom of God among them. The lively discussions lit fires of hope in the hearts of these downtrodden people.

CHAPTER 5

Although I decided I would accept Jesus's invitation to join his ministry, I recognized there were many obstacles to doing so immediately. The initial issue was to whom I would entrust the business my family had built over many years.

After much consideration, I decided to hand the family business over to Sabed. He was very trustworthy and had sufficient experience in our business. So I thought it would be safe in his hands.

Second, I thought about whether Jesus would accept a woman as his close partner. I simply could not decide.

I also thought about my life up to that point. I knew the woman in me desired both motherhood and freedom. Some might see a contradiction in this; I didn't. In fact, I had always tried to give the concept of womanhood a new dimension. For example, I didn't believe it was necessary for a woman to be a mother. That's one reason I remained unmarried. I also had always rejected with contempt the haughtiness men displayed toward women. I had never liked people full of pretension and undue pride.

Also, from my very early childhood on, I believed a woman with determination and moral strength was within me. Yet it's also true I first felt carnal pleasure with a person of my own sex. I wondered if this was a sin, and that possibility tormented me. But I also wasn't a woman who had ever seduced men or exhibited lewd behavior.

I had never been arrogant either. On all occasions, I acted normally and without ego. I also didn't praise people excessively. I believed those qualities gave me an ability to exert influence over other people. I think the circumstances in which I had been brought up and the blessings of God were responsible for these special traits in my character.

It felt uncomfortable to think about myself in such detail. However, I did so in the belief that it might be useful as a means of understanding my mental growth over time. I sum up what I discovered about myself this way: My love of freedom and my intellectualism were quite different from most women in those days.

Thinking all this through ultimately provided a perspective that persuaded me to travel a path full of adventures and to do whatever I could to uplift humanity. This meant I needed to know more about Jesus, so that I could gain his confidence and participate in his ministry—which focused on spreading the message of God.

As I was engaging in such thoughts, Jesus sent me a message through Jacob as he was leaving the villages on the banks of the Jordan River to travel to Capernaum. He expressed the hope that I would follow him on his pilgrimage. I decided to work with him.

***

I traveled to Capernaum, and when I met up with Jesus there, he greeted me with the words "Mary, have you received my message?"

"Yes. Jacob stayed with me for two days—"

"What have you to say?" Jesus asked as he drew me nearer to him and slowly patted my head with his fingers.

"Since I am a woman and not married, there is resentment among some of your followers about me joining the ministry," I said, my torment over this news evident in the tone of my voice.

"Mary, the fact that you are an unmarried woman does not in any way disqualify you from serving God. To face the challenges in front of us, we need the strength of everybody. So let us pray now."

Then we prayed together.

***

Capernaum was a small town near the seashore. More aptly, it was a big village. Most of the people in it were sons of the soil. Jesus called upon them to repent, because the arrival of God's kingdom was imminent.

***

In the beginning, there were only two disciples in Jesus's ministry: Peter and his brother Andrew. It was by sheer coincidence that both became disciples of Jesus.

One evening while Jesus was walking along the beach, he saw those two hefty fishermen throwing their nets into the sea to catch fish. Suddenly, there were high winds and roaring waves. As it was apparent the small boat in which the two men were sitting might capsize and float away at any moment, the brothers tried hard to anchor their boat. Since they were experienced at doing this, they managed to, but in the doing lost their nets and their day's catch. Disappointed, the men sat down on the beach while casting a desolate look into the endless sea.

"Come after me; I will teach you how to catch men!" Jesus commanded.

As if attracted to him by some superhuman power, the two decided right then and there to follow Jesus.

Later, on various occasions, others decided to join Jesus's ministry: Jacob and his brother John; Philip; Bartholomew; Thomas; Alka's son (not the Alka of my house), Jacob; Daddai; Simon; Matthew; and Judas, the man who would betray Jesus.

***

While we were camping in Capernaum, we conducted our lives this way in Jesus's ministry: We got up early each morning. After the daily cleansing of our bodies, we all met in a tent specially erected for a prayer time. After we prayed, Jesus sat on tree bark placed in the middle of the tent. The disciples gathered around him, and he gave out advice.

About praying, Jesus said to us, "When you pray, do not use a lot of meaningless words. Pray that his holy name be honored; may your kingdom come; may your will be done as it is in heaven; give us the food we need; forgive us all the wrongs we have done; and do not bring us to hard testing, but keep us safe from the evil ones."

The disciples of Jesus would explain the gist of what Jesus said about prayer in general to the ordinary folks in the villages. The common people would listen attentively and draw inspiration from the words.

Afterward, we had breakfast. Our meal consisted of bread and wine, and sometimes dried dates.

Daddai was the disciple in charge of meals. However, only Joann and I had the financial means to meet the heavy expense of feeding a large congregation of about forty people each day.

Joann was a woman of extraordinary administrative ability. She was married to Chuza, a wealthy retainer to King Antipas. Like me, she had been possessed by evil spirits once. She too had suffered enormously until Jesus set her free. From that day on, she had dedicated her life to Jesus's ministry. Fearing retribution from Antipas due to this choice, Chuza disowned his wife. However, while leaving her, he gave her a large quantity of gold coins for her to live on comfortably the rest of her life. Together Joann and I oversaw the daily expenses and administrative chores to the best of our ability.

After the morning routine, Jesus and the disciples went around the town, talking to the village people. Jesus wanted to hear of and understand the difficulties of landless peasants.

At noon, it became very hot outside, so it was a time to rest. Some of us would catch a brief nap during that break. In the evening, we resumed our talking tour of the town. On the way, we stopped at previously designated spots to address the townspeople assembled there. Jesus would then talk to them. Most days, around fifty or sixty people gathered to listen to Jesus talk. After a day of hard work, they were anxious to hear what this new prophet had to say that would give them solace.

The disciples always provided some flavor to our talking tour for the townspeople to enjoy. Daddai knew how to make and play a percussion instrument similar to a drum, so throughout Jesus's talk, he would play it with a stick. This often attracted onlookers.

Bartholomew and Thomas had musical talents, and perhaps some formal training in music. So whenever they got the chance, they made Jesus's prophecies into hymns and sang them in front of people.

In return, the public showed respect and generosity to us as we took great pains to spread the gospel.

***

How Matthew became Jesus's disciple is interesting.

Capernaum was situated on the border between the kingdoms of Antipas and his half-brother Philip. There was a huge tax collector's office in the center of the town, and the highest official in the place was a man named Levi.

Several chairs and small tables were on the veranda in front of the office. Many of the tax collectors would sit in these chairs in rapt attention as their minions took the weights and measurements of the tradable items carried in by farmers and traders. They then passed this information over to their tax collector.

In most cases, the tax collector would determine an arbitrary amount as the tax. Only after paying the huge sum would the farmer or trader be allowed to leave Capernaum. Roman soldiers always roamed around the place, maintaining order, despite the arbitrary nature of the taxes.

One day, Joann and I were out searching for Jesus. We finally found him in the tax collector's office, talking in a loud voice to an officer. We watched from a short distance away to allow Jesus to finish his conversation without interruption.

The officer Jesus was addressing was wearing a turban with gold and silver laces and some expensive-looking attire. The man was looking down into the thick book in front of him, pointing at a page. Then he said something to Jesus, as if to justify his actions.

"You do not like this job, do you?" Jesus asked him in a somewhat loud voice.

"Whether I like it or not, this is my task," the man replied in a disappointed tone.

"Levi, this is not a task that appeals to your tribe," Jesus said. Then he moved closer to Levi and said in a pleasant tone, "They are born to serve God. Don't you know that?"

"I have no interest in going to Jerusalem to sit there and pray," Levi replied, laughing.

"You are interested only in making money by abetting crime?" Jesus asked in a stern voice. Then he turned and left.

Joann and I watched Levi sit there silently, his head bowed for a while, before we followed after Jesus.

Later that day, when the sun was coming down, Levi came to our tent and told Jesus he wanted to join our ministry. He said he had made his decision, and it was to dedicate his entire life to God's work.

Jesus blessed him and called him by a new name, Matthew.

***

Whenever possible, Jesus found answers to the questions posed to him by the disciples. He hoped to eliminate any anxieties or worries on their part this way.

Sometimes the cleansing process took the form of questions and answers, as in the conversation I am about to relate.

"Jesus, what is our mission?" asked Bartholomew one day.

"We should destroy Satan, who oppresses the ordinary people. That should be our mission," Jesus answered.

"What should we do in this regard?" asked Philip.

"We should work in unison. I will tell you the details as circumstances warrant," Jesus promised.

Jesus always urged, "Follow me!" with grace and dignity. In those words, his confidence was evident. His disciples understood him.

***

I wished to learn from Jesus in close proximity. He gave me the freedom to approach him whenever I wanted and to ask him whatever questions I needed to ask. But I wasn't sure about the nature of my love toward him or his affection toward me.

One thing was certain though: I was able to visualize him beautifully and completely in my mind. Jesus was a tall man with thick black hair matted down at the back and a face that shined with inner peace. He always dressed in the attire of a peasant, as he himself was interested in simple living. This was the picture I kept of him in my heart and in my mind.

***

All the qualities Jesus possessed suited him to mix best with ordinary folks. He always talked to people in a simple style, although sometimes this led to heated exchanges.

One day, during the course of a talk on the kingdom of God, Jesus observed, "You [the people] are always dear to Father in heaven! He is *your* Father. You should go to him with the same sincerity as a child goes to its father. There is no need for rituals or offerings."

"This is blasphemy!" screeched a middle-aged woman among the attendees at Jesus's talk.

"No, certainly not," Jesus replied in a firm voice. "God desires kindness, not sacrificial lambs or silver coins. Be kind to others. Those who do receive kindness in return." He paused and then continued, "The arrival of God's kingdom is imminent. It's open to you. You must decide for yourself whether you want to enter there or not. If you make your heart ready, it will happen at this very moment!"

Another woman asked loudly, "Is not purity mentioned in Moses's laws?"

"Sister, purity and laws are necessary; I agree. But they are not enough. Are you showing kindness toward your brothers and sisters? Are you extending a helping hand to them if they have a need?" Then he noted in a quiet but clear tone, "A main qualification to enter the kingdom of God is this."

***

One evening, while Jesus and his disciples were staying in Capernaum, a tall, hefty man came to see him. He introduced himself as a battalion commander of the Israeli army.

Jesus received him warmly, and asked, "What help do you need from me?"

"Respected sir, my teenage son is in bed due to a stroke. I can't relate to you the extreme pain he is experiencing. You must kindly cure his illness," the officer implored.

"I will come to your house and make him well."

"Oh no, sir!" responded the officer. "I do not deserve the honor of having you come to my house. Just give the order, and my son will be cured of his illness. You see, I am a high-ranking army officer. There are many soldiers under my command. They will obey my orders, and God will obey yours."

When Jesus heard this, he was surprised. He said to the people around him, "I tell you, I have never found anyone in Israel with faith like this." He turned to the officer. "Go home, and what you believe will be done for you."

The officer's son was healed at that very moment. We heard later that he got up that very day and walked.

***

When people learned about Jesus's ministry in Galilee and Capernaum, they were excited. They crowded around him just to see him or to touch his cloak and thus attain salvation.

One time on a Sabbath day after sunset, the native people brought a middle-aged deaf and blind man before Jesus. Those accompanying the man said he lived in dire poverty; he was the only supporter of his family.

I looked at the man and saw that his furrowed face and famished body were trembling.

"Do you believe that I can heal you?" Jesus asked.

"Yes, Master!" the blind man answered.

Jesus stood there for a few seconds, looking straight into the man's face without blinking his eyes. Then he touched the man's eyes and said in a firm voice, "Let it happen now as you believe."

Immediately, the poor man's sight and hearing were restored.

Not knowing how to express his heartfelt thanks to Jesus, the man bent down to touch Jesus's feet.

"Dedicate your life to God. You are blessed," Jesus said to the man.

The people present that day were amazed at the miracle.

***

It took some time for news of Jesus's mission to reach the ears of John the Baptist, who was in prison at that time. That was because in those days, King Antipas and the Roman authorities had spies everywhere. We believers would exchange messages only through trusted intermediaries.

One day, a few of John's closest disciples came to Jesus and asked, "Are you the Savior of people? Or should we wait for the arrival of another?"

Jesus answered with this short speech: "Blind people get their sight; the dumb hear; the lame walk; the dead are resurrected. The gospel is spreading among the poorest of poor. You all hear and see these things. Let John know about them."

After John's disciples left, Jesus asked his followers, "You often go to the nearby deserts to see what? To see leaves moving in the wind? Or to see a man wearing attire made of expensive cloth? Such people live in kings' palaces, not in deserts." Jesus stopped for a second before he continued. "If you ask me, I will say we went there to see a prophet who is great among the greatest of all prophets—a man who is God's messenger. He is my guide, this John who has baptized many thousands. So far, there is no one born to a woman who is greater than John. This is the truth."

The news of John's imprisonment made Jesus very distraught. He had known that King Antipas was scheming to imprison John for a long time. But Antipas had realized the people would be angered if he did, and so he had waited until then.

Jesus believed that Antipas would not hesitate to imprison even him if he ever got a chance. So believing that his days were numbered, Jesus wanted to go home to Nazareth to spend a day there with his mother and brother.

Only Jesus and I went to Nazareth from Capernaum. This way, we thought we could keep his visit to Nazareth a secret from the prying eyes of Antipas's spies.

Nazareth was in a hilly area, so the trip there was tiresome. Fortunately, we reached there before sunset. It was a midsize village with forty or fifty houses. From the main path, a feeder road went half a mile to the right. Jesus's house was at the end of this road.

The home was well-kept, with its walls painted white and a well in front. It was one of the better homes among the many there.

When we arrived, Jesus's elder brother, James, was talking to a worker in the front yard. Jesus paused to offer his brother, whom he hadn't seen for some time, his greetings.

Then Jesus and I entered the house. We walked past a small reception room and arrived at a courtyard.

This was the first time I'd met Jesus's mother, Miriam. I thought her to be a dignified jewel of a woman. There was kindness in her eyes, and her lips blossomed into a beautiful smile when she saw her son. Although she was approaching old age, she was full of energy.

Mother Miriam received us both warmly. Her words to us reflected love and sincerity.

Jesus introduced me to his mother in this way: "This is Mary, my disciple from Magdala."

She didn't inquire more about it, and said instead, "Oh, my son, at least now you have come to see us." She kissed him on the forehead.

James had entered too, and he asked Jesus many things about his future course of action. But Jesus only promised he would answer later.

It was getting late at night. We ate the food, prepared in the Jewish tradition, and went to bed.

The next day, after saying farewell to his mother and brother, Jesus returned to Galilee, and I went with him.

CHAPTER 6

Jesus was particular in that at least once a week, he had to retreat to a lonely place to mediate. On one of those days, while Jesus was away from Galilee and meditating, Judas Iscariot appeared near our tent.

He was a tall young man with a lean frame and a small beard. He seemed to open and shut his eyes often, as if he had a neurological disorder. His cap was slightly larger than his head, so his forehead was only barely visible. His left hand was busy most of the time, adjusting his cap back up, but not always with success.

Iscariot saw Peter first and introduced himself to him. "I have come to seek the blessings of John the Baptist," he said. "Only on my arrival here did I learn of another man, named Jesus, is going around villages spreading the same message as John's. So I thought of seeing him too. Hence my arrival."

"Jesus is not here now," Peter replied with some indifference. "So you can't see him today."

"Then I shall come tomorrow," Judas replied.

"If you like, you can stay with us today," Jacob said, welcoming the man who would betray Jesus.

That night Jacob and Judas held a long conversation about the kingdom of God as prophesied by Jesus. Judas ended up arguing with Jacob, saying that there was nothing novel in the teachings of Jesus or John the Baptist. He thought the laws of Moses were more far-reaching, and he expressed his clear preference for them.

Even Jacob, who normally didn't speak ill of others, didn't say anything good about Judas after their dialogue.

Jesus returned the same night.

The next day, after the morning prayer, Jesus held a series of discussions with Judas on various topics. This lasted until noon. Since no one else participated in them, none of us knew what the two had discussed. I remember, though, that Jesus postponed that day's tour into town so he could continue that discussion.

When Judas finally was ready to depart, Jesus said to him, "You will always be one of my important disciples, and you have a mission to fulfill. It will unfold in due course."

Saying this, Jesus blessed him. Thus Judas Iscariot became the twelfth apostle of Jesus.

***

Although the folks in the villages around Galilee were generally poor and illiterate, their belief in and respect for the laws of Moses were absolute. They also held their religious leaders in high esteem. Jesus brought a new covenant—not a physical covenant like Moses's, but the covenant of God. He called sinners to repent and thus attain salvation. But Jesus didn't adhere strictly to the laws of Moses himself; he even transgressed some, including laws pertaining to the Sabbath. In the matter of purity, Jesus opposed the law of God as given to Moses by declaring all foods clean. In fact, he was autonomous; he interpreted the law according to his own rules. This made it difficult for ordinary people to understand his messages fully. However, even in Galilee, where the people didn't understand or accept us, we carried on our ministry with vigor.

As it turned out, the Pharisees were afraid of the village folks of Galilee who showed interest in Jesus and his message, because the Galileans thought of him as *their* Savior. The Pharisees believed the ordinary people's belief posed a serious threat to their supremacy in society, and so they connived to stop Jesus's activities in any way possible.

To this end, they continually hatched several plots. On occasion, a Pharisee would ask Jesus questions on different topics. At times, this might go on in the synagogues. Most people knew well that the Pharisees were doing this to discredit Jesus and to create impediments to his ministry. But Jesus never showed any anger or disrespect toward them.

One day, two Pharisees followed Jesus as he was returning from speaking to people in a synagogue. They began to ask him questions. "Master, we would like you to make a sign regarding the arrival of the kingdom of God. Can you do that?" one of the Pharisees asked him cautiously.

Jesus thought for a while before he replied, "An angry generation that indulges in prostitution is seeking a sign. You will not get anything other than the sign of the prophet Yona."

Another day, Jesus was having his meal while sitting on a blanket on the floor. There were disciples on both sides of him, including me. As he ate, three or four tax collectors were passing through the village where we were staying. Upon hearing of Jesus's presence, they came over to us and sat among the disciples. They said they were tired and hungry, so we fed them also. Relieved, they said thanks to Jesus and left with his blessings.

Some Pharisees came to know about this event, so the next time they saw Jacob at the beach, they asked him why his master was partaking his meal with "sinners and tax collectors, who harass people."

When Jacob mentioned this question to Jesus, at first Jesus only smiled. After a short while, he said to his disciples, "Only a patient needs a doctor, not healthy people. Those who came here were hungry and needed food. Let them be anybody. To give them food is my obligation. Go tell the Pharisees I am pleased to show mercy, and I am not like the Pharisees, who are pleased by rites in the temple. I am here to minister to sinners, not to righteous people."

***

John the Baptist was still in prison, and he and his disciples had come to know about Jesus's activities. Because his followers were unable to be in direct contact with John because of his imprisonment, they would come to Jesus with their questions. Whenever they came, they always brought dried fruit, bread, or other things as signs of love and respect.

One day, John's disciples came to Jesus and inquired, "Master, fasting according to the laws of Moses is an integral part of purifying the body. Then why are your disciples not fasting?"

Jesus received them properly, then said calmly, "When the groom is with them, his relatives cannot grieve. A day will come when he leaves; on that day they will fast. Nobody stitches a new piece of cloth to an old dress; this will destroy the beauty of the new cloth. New wine is not poured into an old pot; it will overflow, and the pot will get dirty. New wine should be poured into a new pot. Thus both wine and pot will be safe."

Since John's disciples nodded, we thought they understood the point Jesus was trying to make.

While Jesus and John's disciples were talking like this, a prominent man from the village came and prostrated himself before Jesus. His face was fraught with grief, and he pleaded in a humble tone, "Master, by now my daughter is dead. However, if you touch her, she will live."

Hearing this, Jesus proceeded to the man's house with a few of his followers without any hesitation. When he got there, he discovered that the distraught man had arranged for a small band with musical instruments. There were also singers present. Jesus ignored them all and went straight to the room where the little girl was lying on a bed.

"Your daughter is not dead. She is sleeping," Jesus announced.

Hearing this, the people gathered there thought he was mad. They laughed derisively at his words.

But Jesus went near the girl, held her hands, and gently commanded, "Little girl, get up!"

And the girl got up!

Due to what had just happened, the people standing outside began to sing and dance in merriment. They cried out many times in unison, "Hosanna! You are the son of God!"

The band played all night long.

While Jesus was returning to our tent, two blind men followed him. "Oh, son of David! Please have mercy on us, and give us our sight!" they begged.

"Do you believe I have the ability to give you sight?" Jesus asked.

"Certainly, our Lord, you can," both said in loud voices.

Touching their eyes, Jesus said, "Let it happen as you believe."

Miraculously, both men opened their eyes and were able to see.

Jesus's reputation as a healer spread far and wide. This attracted huge crowds wherever he went. The authorities thought this would create political difficulties for them, so they viewed Jesus's activities with suspicion.

Jesus told his disciples not to tell of this to anybody, and the disciples obeyed.

***

Hearing about the missionary work Jesus was carrying out in Galilee, the religious leaders and Pharisees in Jerusalem became angry. They hatched a secret plan to destroy his ministry.

As part of this plan, two heavyset Pharisees showed up one day at our prayer tent and expressed their desire to converse with Jesus. He agreed; he never refused such encounters.

"You can ask me whatever you want," Jesus said them in a humble tone.

"Why are your disciples not following our ancestors? One example is that they do not wash their hands before their meals." They moved close to Jesus, as if very much interested in knowing his answer.

Jesus responded, "Why are you violating God's commandments by your actions? God has commanded that fathers and mothers should be respected, and those who malign them should die. What about you? If anyone gives you an offering of ten talents,[2] their sins are forgiven, and they do not have to respect their parents. In your scheme, God's sayings are weak."

Then Jesus said to the other people present, "These Pharisees complain that we do not wash our hands and cleanse ourselves before our meals. There is no meaning in this. It's not what goes into the mouth that makes a man unclean, it's what comes out."

Hiding their anger, the Pharisees left hastily without waiting to hear more.

Upon hearing from the disciples that the Pharisees had left unconvinced, Jesus continued, "All those not planted by my Father in heaven will be destroyed at their roots. Let it be so. They are like blind people showing the way. If a blind person shows the way, both will fall into the hole."

When Peter heard this parable, he implored Jesus to explain this a

---

[2] A coin in Israel at that time.

bit more. Jesus smiled and said, "Don't you know whatever we put in the mouth comes out when we go to the toilet? But whatever comes out of the mouth is from the heart. That is what makes a man unclean. From inside the heart come evil ideas that lead him to do unusual things. Eating without washing hands does not make one unclean."

When the disciples heard this explanation, they were satisfied.

On one occasion, a Pharisee spread a disgusting rumor in a hilly area where a tribe known as Gadere resided. He told the people that Jesus was releasing demons with the help of Beelzebub, the leader of demons.

Peter learned about this allegation one day and informed Jesus about it. Jesus tried to explain away the allegation made by the annoyed Pharisees with another parable: "If there is internal strife in one country, who will perish? If a town or a house has internal strife, it will not stand. If Satan's kingdom divides into groups, it cannot stand, but will fall apart and come to an end. If I am getting out demons with Beelzebub's help, your children will ask, 'Whose help?' If I am getting rid of the evil spirits, believe that the arrival of God's kingdom is imminent."

***

One early morning, Jesus left the tent for the beach, where he sat silently. Hearing about his arrival there, several hundred people gathered. The speech he gave to them that day was also strewn with parables.

Jesus said, "A man went out to sow grain. As he scattered the seeds in the field, some of it fell along the path, and birds ate it up. Some of it fell on rocky ground, where there was little soil. The seed soon sprouted, because the soil wasn't deep. But when the sun came up, it burned the young plants, and because the roots hadn't grown deep enough, the plants soon dried up.

"Some of the seeds fell among thorn bushes, which grew up and choked the plants, so they didn't bear grain. But some of the seeds fell in good soil, and the plants sprouted and grew and bore grain. Some had sixty; others, a hundred-and-fifty seeds of grain."

Jesus concluded by asking the group to listen to his words.

Jacob, the most thoughtful of all the disciples, asked Jesus to explain a bit more of what he had said. He always tried to understand the inner meaning of new ideas; only then was he satisfied.

Jesus answered him in this way: "You now have an opportunity to understand the core principles underlying the kingdom of God. Others don't have this. He who has will be given more; he will prosper.

"From he who does not have, whatever he has will be taken away. Others may look, yet not see; they may listen, yet not understand. I speak to them in parables, so they can see and understand; for if they did, they would turn to God and he would forgive them."

On the same day, Jesus told yet another parable: "The kingdom of God is like this: A man scattered wheat seeds in his field. As he slept at night, the enemy came and sowed bad seeds among the good. While the seeds were sprouting and growing, the man did not know what happened. First, the tender stalks appeared, then the heads, and finally, the heads full of grain. But the bad seed also grew. The servant went to the owner and asked him, 'Lord, have not you spread good seed in the field? Then how come weeds grew up among them?'"

"'The enemy did this,' the owner replied.

"'Should we go out and remove the weeds?' the agitated servant inquired.

"'No,' answered the owner. 'When you pull out the weeds, the wheat stalks also will be destroyed. So let both grow. When the harvest season comes, we will ask the threshers to cut the bad stalks separately and burn them. Then they can remove the good wheat and store it in the grain room."

Again Jacob asked Jesus to explain the meaning of his latest parable. Jesus was happy to oblige, saying, "The man who sowed good seed is the son of God; the field is the world; the good seed, the people; the weed, the children of Satan; those who sow bad seed, Satan; and those who harvest, the messengers. Just as the weeds are gathered up and burned in fire, the same thing will happen at the end of the age."

Jacob and his friends liked that parable very much.

Jesus also compared the kingdom of heaven to a mustard seedling in another parable. "One man took mustard seed and put it in the field. Though the seed was small compared to that of other plants, it grew to full size. So all the birds came to roost on the branches."

Hearing this, the ordinary people were amazed. They wondered from where Jesus had gotten all this knowledge.

***

Jesus's disciples, separately and jointly, enthusiastically carried on his missionary work. They traveled among the common people and tried to understand their problems firsthand. As Jesus ordained, the disciples were able to make the ordinary folks more aware of the coming of God's kingdom.

***

As Jesus suspected, and due to pressure exerted by the priesthood, Antipas accelerated his plan to imprison Jesus. Hearing of this, Jesus decided to go a second time to Nazareth to stay with his family for a day or two. From among the disciples, he invited only me to accompany him. I considered this a great honor.

Before leaving for Nazareth, Jesus called all his disciples into his presence. He gave them authority to drive off evil spirits and to heal every disease. He instructed them with these words: "You are going out to the lost sheep of the people of Israel. Go and preach, 'The kingdom of heaven is real!'

"Heal the sick, bring the dead back to life, and drive out demons. You have received without paying, so give without being paid. If some home or town will not welcome you or listen to you, leave that place and shake its dust off your feet."

Our travel to Nazareth proved difficult, as it always did. The terrain was full of ups and downs, the main path littered with holes and wet soil. Only with extreme caution could we proceed.

When we finally reached Jesus's home, Mother Miriam and Jesus's brother James received us warmly. However, James didn't hide his fear or anxiety about Jesus's situation. "Who will conduct the family trade?" he wondered aloud. "And, Jesus, why incur the enmity of the priesthood by talking about the kingdom of God in synagogues? How can you walk among the people with your head up?"

Hearing James's worries, Mother Miriam moved even closer to Jesus with an affectionate smile. She was always like that: kind and affectionate.

"I am listening to the call of God the Almighty," Jesus said calmly.

"That is my duty hereafter. Whether you, my mother, and my brother want to join me in my ministry work is up to you to decide."

"Jesus, you must decide your own affairs," James responded. "I would like to fulfill my family responsibilities."

To me, the conversation between the two brothers seemed incomplete. I felt Jesus didn't try his best to let his brother know of God's commandments. But after all, Jesus was also human.

CHAPTER 7

From Nazareth, Jesus went to Sidon. He continued his ministry there by curing the ill and giving sight to the blind and hearing to the deaf. From Galilee all the way through to distant Syria, people heard about his divine powers and were saying, "This is the son of God." All praised him.

The Roman authorities and King Antipas thought Jesus's activities were a threat to their supremacy. To this end, Antipas filled the country with spies to monitor his activities.

The rumor that the authorities had decided to put Jesus in prison when they found him spread far and wide. So he continued to keep his movements as secret as possible. He gave his disciples and the general public strict instructions not to trumpet any deeds he performed, like curing the sick or giving alms to the poor. The simple folks of Galilee followed those instructions to the letter.

***

One day, Thaddeus, our main cook, told us the heart-wrenching story of the sad demise of John the Baptist. That tragic event unfolded like this.

In those days, Herod Antipas ruled a portion of Judea; his half-brother Philip ruled another. As briefly mentioned in an earlier chapter, neither possessed personal integrity. Nor did they have any power of their own; both were mere puppets in the hands of Pontius Pilate, the procurator of the Roman emperor in Judea.

King Antipas developed a love for his half-brother's wife, the most beautiful Herodias. He wanted to make her his wife. Many people counseled Antipas that this was wrong, but he didn't listen to them. Eventually Antipas managed to make Herodias his queen.

John the Baptist was one of those who counseled Antipas against giving in to this lust. Because of this, Antipas incarcerated him. Although he wanted to kill John immediately, he hesitated from carrying out that devilish plot because of John's popularity among the common people.

For Antipas's next birthday, Herodias gave an elaborate banquet in honor of the king. Like any other conniving queen in those days, she concocted a plan to achieve her wish to marry Antipas. The banquet was outstanding and attended by many high-ranking dignitaries, the ministers of Antipas, and senior military officers.

Herodias had arranged for her extremely beautiful and talented daughter to dance at the banquet. Pleased at the young girl's outstanding performance, Antipas vowed he would give her any gift she wanted. Upon the advice of her mother, the daughter requested that the king give her the head of John the Baptist in a golden vase.

Hearing this, Antipas became nervous, because he had not yet settled on a plan to kill John. However, he decided he could not violate the promise he had made at the banquet in front of so many dignitaries. So he secretly issued an order that John be killed, in order to fulfill his promise. In secret, he then gave John's head in the golden vase to Herodias's daughter. And she gave it to her mother.

Somehow John's disciples came to know of this. They entered Herodias's chamber in the palace in secret and took possession of the head, then buried it with the proper rites.

Upon hearing the details of John's death, we all grieved, and especially Jesus. His intense sorrow left dark shadows on his face for weeks.

Yet another sinister rumor soon surfaced in Galilee: Jesus was the resurrected John the Baptist, and that was why he had the rare blessing of being able to cure the sick. The rumor also gave Antipas one more reason to want Jesus imprisoned.

All of us in Jesus's ministry took care to be extremely cautious.

***

Once we were traveling through the land ruled by Antipas's half-brother

Philip. It was a Roman district composed of small towns on the eastern shore of the Sea of Galilee.

We got down onto the beach from the boat and walked a short distance. The land was deserted. Many scattered rock formations jutted above the water close to land. When there was high wind and hail, powerful waves crashed hard on those rocks, scattering water everywhere. So even the poor fishermen lived far off the beach for reasons of safety.

I watched Jesus as he walked along with his cane, head bowed and deep in thought. The rays of the setting sun cast down his long, thin shadow. I could discern that the death of John the Baptist had left a deep wound in his soul.

Suddenly, all of us present heard a bloodcurdling cry. At first, we didn't know where it came from. Jesus stopped to look around.

A naked man appeared in front of us from behind one of the big rocks. He was so dirty, he didn't look like a human.

The strong-looking man stood in front of us and hollered ferociously. His filthy hair stood up in tufts; foam flew out of his mouth; and his eyes were bloodshot. He brandished a sharp stone in one hand, and there were manacles on his wrists. He obviously had been restrained and somehow broken apart the chains that had bound him.

Peter said we should run for our safety. Although he was a sturdy man, obviously he didn't feel ready to subdue this madman. "He's dangerous! He'll kill anyone who faces him directly!" Peter warned, trying to drag Jesus away.

The beast of a man decided to confront Jesus, the leanest among us. Roaring and jumping up and down, the man kept running in circles around Jesus. Then his roaring became only a faint cry.

Before the man could make another sound, Jesus commanded, "Come out of this man, you ghastly demon!"

"Jesus, if you won't hurt me, I will come out of this man," promised an unfamiliar voice. The man ceased his fearsome jumps and no longer ran about. He sat crouched at Jesus's feet.

"What is your name?" Jesus asked in a stern tone.

"Legion." The man slowly raised his head, wiped away the foam coming out of his mouth, and added, "For we are many."

Jesus raised his voice and ordered the legion of demons, "Leave this man!"

"Where will we go?" said the voice from the man, who was now moaning and groaning as well.

"Who will give us refuge?"

"To hell! That is where I am sending you," Jesus replied in a grave voice.

The man suddenly fell to the ground and didn't move from the spot.

Daddai gave the man his bread; Peter, his sandals; and Philip, his extra gown. When the man seemed somewhat recovered and rational, we sent him away as Jesus told him, "God saved you. Always remember that, and if you can, try to spread his name among your tribe."

While the man was reverentially taking leave of us, Jesus blessed him and called him Joshua.

***

It was an unusually hot day. People were gathered around our tent even as the sun was rising in the sky. They all wanted to see Jesus and receive his blessing.

As usual, when he came out after his morning prayer, they started asking him questions, one after another. They wanted his advice on everything, and this was a time when the ordinary people were angry about the rule of a foreign power—the Romans—over them.

"Master, you yourself must tell us. The Romans are ruling over us. Is it just and right to give them taxes?" A Pharisee had raised this question, and he moved a step forward, as if ready to listen intently to what Jesus had to say.

The man's true intent probably was to provoke Jesus. You see, the extremist Jews among us were firmly against paying taxes to the Roman emperor; the authorities had branded these extremists as seditious. The moderates among us favored paying taxes, but the common people declared that any who took that position to be cowards. So, on the subject of paying taxes, there was no consensus among the people. Under the circumstances, any opinion Jesus offered about paying taxes might prove divisive. His response might make him less appealing to one group and thereby adversely affect his missionary work.

"Give me a coin," were Jesus's first words when the Pharisee finished speaking.

Someone standing nearby gave Jesus a Roman denarius. He looked carefully at both sides of the coin. Then he raised his head, handed the coin to the Pharisee who had raised the question, and asked, "Whose picture do you see?"

The Pharisee cleaned the dirty coin with a piece of cloth. Then he looked at it and replied, "Tiberius Caesar."

"Then give whatever is Caesar's to Caesar and whatever is God's to God," Jesus answered.

The majority of people assembled there didn't know the meaning of that statement.

"Why should we pay taxes to Caesar?" Jacob asked impatiently.

"All those laws are temporary. In God's kingdom there is no relevance for such questions. So we should not waste our time on them," Jesus counseled.

Everybody agreed with what Jesus said, and the crowd dispersed.

***

The Romans had their soldiers deployed even in small towns. The authorities had given these soldiers strict instructions not to interfere in the affairs of Jews, who were peaceful and law-abiding. However, on occasion, they created unnecessary troubles for the people.

Around the time of the Pharisee's question of Jesus, the secret soldiers of Sikri mounted an attack on the Roman's army base in Sore. This was in retaliation for the abduction and killing of one of their warriors. The attack was mounted against a base manned by Roman soldiers highly trained in warfare. It proved a failure, and around a hundred Sikri warriors perished in the attack. Those who survived waited for an opportunity to exact revenge.

One day, a battalion of Roman soldiers was marching toward Jerusalem. As the sun began to set, they reached a village about six miles from Jerusalem. Their captain, Dimitrian, ordered them to stop and stay overnight in the village.

This captain was from an illustrious military family from Rome, and he was arrogant by temperament. He also was a distant relative of Pilate, the Roman procurator.

It was the normal procedure of the Romans to bring along the necessary provisions with them on any march. However, for some reason, they needed drinking water. Two soldiers set out from the village to fetch water. The warriors of Sikri, who were hiding nearby, captured them and took them to their base.

When dusk came, and the soldiers had still not returned, Captain Dimitrian became very angry. To find out what happened to his men, he himself set out to the area where the well was located. Ten or twelve of his best soldiers accompanied him to the site.

There near the well, they had dug a hole. On top of it, they had laid bamboo sticks, which they then covered with leaves and dirt.

When the captain arrived with his soldiers, it was dark. The captain and his men fell into the trap laid out for them. The Sikri warriors immediately detained them and took them to their base.

Later they released all the Roman soldiers, except for the captain, whom they cruelly murdered. Not only that, they thrust his head on a spear and sent it to Pilate through a courier.

It was no wonder the Roman authorities redoubled their repressive measures.

***

Winter slowly crept away. Spring came forward with all its charm. We continued our pilgrimage—our destination, Mount Hermon.

The common people we encountered on the way gave us food. Some of them requested Jesus stay with them for at least for a few minutes. They wanted to see the holy man, their Savior.

Jesus never disappointed them.

***

It was my custom to discuss and evaluate my knowledge of and opinions about the Torah and its lessons. I found that in our group were many who knew more about its teachings than I, particularly Jacob and Thomas. From time to time, I would share my thoughts with them.

One day, I asked diffidently, "I would like to know more about these matters. Is not Jesus's approach to certain things rather unclear?"

Jacob made his position known through these words: "I carefully learned Moses's laws in my early childhood. But Jesus's ideas are novel and progressive; we need an open mind to absorb them. It's not possible to analyze anything with preconditions, like everything written in the Torah is sacrosanct. Not only that, Jesus is able to evaluate everything authoritatively."

Thomas opened his mind to me as well. "God's message to us is this: 'I will give my strength to you, and thus you will live.' But I do not know how it will happen. I believe Jesus will show this to us. That is why I became his disciple."

While we were talking, Judas came over and asked us, "What are the topics you are discussing so seriously?"

"We are discussing some general issues like, What are we doing here?" Thomas replied.

"Jesus is always talking about the ultimate objective of this movement, is he not?" Judas said a bit impatiently.

"What is your opinion about what we're doing here?" Jacob asked curtly. He seemed annoyed.

Hiding many things in his mind, Judas continued, "Jesus thinks he knows everything. But the master is leading us to danger. Why incur the hostilities of the authorities?"

"I am also concerned about that," Thomas said in an uneasy tone.

I didn't like the way the conversation was heading. To change the subject, I asked, "How many days are we going to stay in Mount Hermon?"

"That is not decided," Jacob responded.

Thus ended the conversation.

***

Around twelve thousand years ago, Dan was a prosperous and densely populated town on the northern slope of Mount Hermon. It was inhabited by the Dan tribe, one of Israel's twelve tribes, and ruled over by a representative of King Solomon.

The town was destroyed when the Assyrians invaded, and everyone in the Dan tribe perished. Dan grew into a dense forest, where oak and cypress trees abound.

For us to camp in that area, we cleared a small, flat spot on one side of the hill. They made a fire, and we stayed there overnight.

The main reason Jesus had come to Dan was to stay far removed from the prying eyes of the authorities. He wanted to think about and give shape to his future course of action in complete secrecy. He thought Dan would be a good place to do this.

As usual, I settled down to sleep after the evening prayer. A bit of heat from the fire crept over to me as a dusting of snowflakes began to fall. Exhausted, I fell asleep quickly.

The dream I had that night was frightening. In a rather distant town, enraged Roman soldiers were trying to disperse an equally angry mob. The soldiers were stabbing the people with spears, and some of the people were beheaded. A crowd of people holding cressets in their hands began running aimlessly in different directions and screaming something unintelligible. Among them, I saw Jesus, who had blood oozing from several parts of his body. He was trying to say something to a Roman soldier who was trying to handcuff him.

Shaking with fright, I woke up.

It was late in the night. There was darkness everywhere; only a dim light emanated from the campfire. I felt I should inform Jesus about this dream immediately. I knew he always got up very early in the morning to withdraw to an isolated place to mediate. I looked around carefully and managed to spy him walking away from our site. I ran after him.

When I was near Jesus, I reached out and touched his cloak, pleading, "Stop! I have something to say."

"What is it, Mary?" he asked as he turned to me.

My untimely arrival had startled him a bit; I saw that in his look. I said, my voice cracking, "Please let me tell you about a dream I had last night."

"Say," he directed.

"Jerusalem! That is the city I saw," I began. "Roman soldiers, along with Antipas's police, were roaming everywhere and beating people. After—after that I saw you wounded and falling into the hands of a soldier—"

I could not talk anymore because of my intense grief and fright.

"I will die in Jerusalem; that decisive moment is near," Jesus responded. "Mary, I know you cannot face that. However, you should be brave. This is the will of God, our Father in heaven," Jesus said in a peaceful but firm voice.

My eyes filled with tears as the morning sun rose above the eastern hills of Dan, spreading pale-red rays across the sky. Fawns ran here and there past us, full of merriment. Two or three ran over to the stream running on one side of the hill. A huge falcon flew up into the sky after its night's rest.

"Mary, let me tell you. This age is coming to an end. The corruption in the temple and the religious leaders that support it have already been rejected by God." Jesus stopped for a second or two before he continued. "The revelation you had is correct. But its complete picture has not unfolded in me yet."

Jesus took both my hands and pulled me close to him. He said softly, "I am thankful to you for telling me this. I also thank God for revealing it to you."

When Jesus touched me with his hands, my heartbeat quickened, and my heart began to throb. The woman in me raised her head and looked at the prophet's shining face; my lips longed to press against his face.

For a few seconds, Jesus gazed quietly into my sparkling eyes. Then he said softly in a voice tinged with emotion, "Mary, I know you love me."

Seconds! Precious seconds passed us by! I knew not for how long. *Jesus is mine, and I am his.* This he told me; I had no doubt about it.

The scene ended like that.

***

As I wrote earlier, on our return journey to Jerusalem, Jesus and I decided to stay a day or two with his family in Nazareth. *What could happen in the coming days?* I wondered.

Mother Miriam and Jesus's brother James were very happy to see Jesus and me. When she discovered that our next destination was Jerusalem, she embraced her son and said, "Many dangers are waiting to happen. I do not know what they are!"

Upon hearing these words, I became very worried. *Has Mother Miriam had the same revelation as I?*

She directed her next words to me. "The moment Jesus was born,

I knew he had a special mission to perform in this world. He is going to fulfill that now. For that moment I must also be with him. This is a pilgrimage for me as well."

As she finished saying this, she kissed Jesus on the forehead.

The affection a mother has for her son!

James came forward and expressed his desire to accompany Mother Miriam to Jerusalem. Jesus agreed to it.

CHAPTER 8

Jesus chose to discuss only with Peter bits of information about his future course of action. The disciples were anxious to know what was going to happen in Jerusalem. They were about to challenge an extremely powerful administrative machine, and some of them were uneasy about it. But whatever the consequences, they didn't want to desert Jesus.

On the way to Jerusalem, we encountered a woman with a jar full of water. Jesus went to her and asked, "Woman, could you give me some water to drink?"

"Is not even talking to each other forbidden?" she asked, looking suspiciously at Jesus.

He answered calmly while holding out a leather pouch, "Yes, and please pour some into my bag."

The Samaritan woman gave water to Jesus and his followers as she said, "Drinking water from the same pot must be even worse than our speaking with each other!"

"Woman, if you know God's grace, you will realize who is asking for water to drink. Then you will ask me for water," Jesus replied, laughing. "For that you do not have a big enough leather bag to draw water from the well."

Eyeing Jesus suspiciously, the woman took a step back.

He said, "People who drink water from your well will get thirsty again. But those who drink the water I give will get everlasting life. They will never be thirsty again."

"Great man, you may be a prophet, but we, the people of Samaria, worship the God of Mount Gerizim. Jews say their temple is in Jerusalem. Why is it so?" she asked.

"Without delay, a day will come when there will be no prayer in both these places. God is self-realization. The temple is where those who are able to distinguish this gather," Jesus informed her in a friendly voice.

"We all know the Savior is coming soon. When he appears before us, he may explain these matters to us," the woman said with hope.

"Women, I am the Savior you are waiting anxiously for."

The wonderstruck woman stood there for a few seconds. Then she ran to the main town square. On the way she came upon a traveler to whom she described the encounter she'd just had with Jesus in all its details. To make it more dramatic, she added some glittering stuff of her own.

In a matter of hours, the majority of the people in Schem, the district headquarters of Samaria, came to know that Jesus and his followers were camped in the vicinity. They gathered near our camp, ready to hear Jesus's message. It was, indeed, a big crowd, and those who came to hear about God's kingdom brought bread and wine with them. This was more than sufficient for our group.

After the meal, Jesus addressed those assembled. Upon hearing his speech, the common people of Samaria were overjoyed, and they left with tears of joy. Some among us felt uneasy about Jesus sharing his meal with the Samaritans, but none of us took it seriously.

We continued our journey the next day and reached Jerusalem around noon on the fourth day. We paused on a hill on the northern side of the city. There we looked at the vast expanse of land before us.

The city of Jerusalem was immersed in bright sunlight, the source of a divine self—and purity. We spied the temple with its golden domes and several beautiful palaces built with pure white marble.

As we traveled down the steps built on one side of the hill, Jesus was overcome with emotion. When he finally stood in front of the temple, his eyes became moist.

The sight of this stunned the disciples. None of us knew what to do.

"Jerusalem! Let there be peace here," Jesus spoke softly, as if to comfort himself.

Mother Miriam, Peter, and the rest of our group moved forward. Singing hymns, we walked toward the main temple door. Since it was

Passover, the temple and its surroundings were filled with pilgrims. On such special occasions, the Roman authorities deployed more soldiers around the temple. But the soldiers stayed outside it.

The tense political environment prevailing at the time in no way reduced the reverence Jews felt for their temple. Nor did it diminish the number of Jews who came to visit it.

***

En route to Jerusalem, Jesus and the disciples had stayed for two days in a village named Bethany, near Olive, as Jesus had quite a few ardent followers there. They told us Jesus was a "marked man" and suggested he stay with them for a time to avoid detection by authorities.

The day after reaching Bethany, Jesus called Daddai to his side and instructed, "Go to the village ahead of us. There you will find a donkey tied in front of a particular house. Bring that donkey to me." When Daddai asked what to do if the owner objected to taking his donkey away, Jesus replied, "Tell him the Master needs it, and the man will let it go at once."

The next day, Jesus went to the temple on the back of the donkey Daddai had brought. Peter walked in front, holding the donkey's reins.

No one said anything. Everybody followed Jesus silently.

In the evening, the authorities opened the huge gate in front of the temple. Jesus and all his disciples except Judas entered along with other pilgrims. Mother Miriam, Joann, and I followed so that we might watch whatever events were to unfold. However, we took care to stay a distance behind.

Everybody was thrown into an uproar. *Surprise!* All looked at Jesus, riding on a donkey. They asked among themselves, in hushed tones, "Who is this energetic and handsome young man?"

They all began to chant, "Praise to David's son! God bless him who comes in the name of the Lord!"

Judas, who was with me, whispered in my ear, "This is fraud."

I hated his words, but I kept silent because of the seriousness of the circumstances. Only two days before, a secret Jewish warrior named Barabbas had killed a Roman soldier. The authorities now had Roman soldiers stationed on top of the walls around the city to control the crowd if necessary.

Daylight started to whitewash the neighborhood. With no advance warning, a middle-aged, voluptuous, long-haired woman showed up in front of the house where we all were staying. She carried a jug with her. Its top was covered with a piece of cloth, so we didn't know what it contained. We were on the alert since Antipas and his people used even women for spying.

Jesus himself was not perturbed. After getting permission, the woman entered the house and went straight over to Jesus, who was about to have breakfast.

With respect and veneration, she poured over him scented oil she had been carrying in the jug. Then she wiped off the oil flowing down his face with a piece of cloth and used the oil remaining in the jug to pour onto his feet. These she began to tenderly massage.

Everybody watched silently. What she did after this really amazed all of us: she wiped away the oil that was flowing over Jesus's body with her splendid curly hair.

I could not figure out what her motivation was in doing this. Even today it remains a mystery to me. I remember only that she let out a faint cry while doing this act.

After wiping the oil away, she stood up, covered her face with one hand, and began to leave. Jesus stopped her by raising his right hand. He got up and moved close to her. Then he reached over and removed the hand from her face. He held onto her hand as he told us, "What she did today is a divine act. She anointed my body with oil, before my burial. Her name shall be remembered in the world forever! I am calling her Mary of Bethany."

Upon hearing these words of her son, Mother Miriam wept.

CHAPTER 9

When Mary of Bethany left, Jesus said to us, "Tomorrow is Passover night. We will have our dinner near the temple; I have made arrangements for that." With complete confidence, he looked at the disciples and continued, "This age is coming to an end. Do not be afraid. The need of the hour is unity among us."

After saying this, he called Daddai to him before he gave instructions: "Daddai is to go to the eastern door of the temple; there he will spot a man carrying a jug full of water. He should follow this man. Since it's unusual for men to carry water in a jug, Daddai should not have any difficulty spotting him.

"When the man reaches a particular house, Daddai should ask the owner of that house to arrange a dinner for the Father in heaven the next day."

Daddai left and did what Jesus asked him to do.

The short stay at Bethany seemed to have reenergized Jesus. When we met for dinner the next night, he welcomed everybody. Then Mother Miriam came forward and whispered something in her son's ear. He shook his head slightly, as if consenting to what his mother had said. "Everybody be seated," he instructed.

Usually Jesus sat at the head of the table. This time he didn't. Instead he sat along one side of the table between Peter and Thomas.

Jesus asked Joann to bring him some warm water in a basin and some towels.

The next thing he did amazed us all. He got up, took off his cloak, and said, "My dear disciples, you are destined to serve others. Those who have should serve those who do not have. I am now going to demonstrate that to you."

He wet a towel with water, bent down, and began to wash Peter's feet.

Peter didn't like this and he hastily got up from his seat. "The Master is washing the feet of a disciple?!" he said.

With a smile, Jesus said to him, "If you do not let me wash your feet, you will not become a part of me."

Hearing this, Peter consented to the washing. Then Jesus went around and washed the feet of everyone sitting at the table.

Finally, he came over to me, washed both of my feet, and wiped them dry. My heart throbbed. *Jesus is bending down, touching my feet like he is a servant!*

After washing the feet of everyone present, he firmly repeated what he had said many times before, but using these words: "Always remember: You are obliged to serve others." Then Jesus put on his cloak and took his usual seat at the head of the table to partake the meal.

Thaddeus, our cook, served grapes and apples from Galilee, and pistachios and dried dates from Syria were placed on the table. Joann served dried fish from Magdala as well as fried eggs, ham, and onions.

Everyone said a special thanks to Thaddeus, our cook, for the feast before us. It was a heavenly treat for the disciples who had eaten lightly while traveling for many years through mountain terrain and deserts. All were in a joyous mood.

Jesus poured red wine into a cup. Raising it, he proclaimed, "This is my blood, which seals God's covenant. My blood is poured out for many for the forgiveness of their sins. I tell you, I will not drink this wine again until the day I drink the new wine with you in my Father's kingdom." He added solemnly, "Whenever you drink wine, remember this is my blood!"

Everybody was silent at these words.

Jesus pronounced suddenly, "One of you will betray me."

These words scared the disciples. They looked around at each other with fear on their countenances.

Thomas and Bartholomew could not believe this to be true.

Peter and John whispered something in Jesus's ears.

Judas looked like he was going to speak, but did not.

Jesus said no more on the topic, and the supper continued. While we all were eating, Jesus took a piece of bread, gave a prayer of thanks, broke the bread, and gave it to his disciples. "Take it, and eat," he said. "This is my body."

After the disciples ate it, Jesus took a piece of bread and dipped it in wine. He then gave it to Judas and said, "Whatever you are going to do, do it soon."

Judas bristled at these words. He pushed away from the table and left in a hurry. Although the other disciples noticed this, only Joann and I knew the real reason for Judas disappearing into the darkness.

After a short while, Jesus made a brief speech: "I am extremely glad that I was able to spend time with you during Passover. I have been hoping for this for a long time. You are the chosen ones. Please listen to what I have to say."

After pausing for a few seconds, he continued, "My children, I will be with you only for a short while. You will certainly search for me, but you will not be able to come to where I am going. However, I am giving you a new command; please listen carefully. *Love each other.* The same way I loved you all, you are to love others. That is how people all over the world will know you are my disciples."

Peter became unsettled and asked, "Master, where are you going? I will also come with you. For the sake of God's kingdom, I am ready for anything—to go to jail or even to give my life."

Jesus replied, "I tell you that before the rooster crows this night, you will disown me three times."

"I will never do that, even if I have to die with you!"

"You are possessed by Satan; that is why you will disown me. However, I have prayed for you, that you will become free. You will now make your brothers and sisters ready for missionary work."

Jesus concluded, "May you all have peace! Now please let me go. I will send the Holy Ghost to you. I know he will protect you. I am going to my Father's presence. Rejoice in that. I will come again."

Jesus looked at each of his disciples and told them they should never be sad when they think about him, but keep happiness in their hearts.

Everybody then sang the hymns.

Probably due to her foreknowledge that some terrible events were going to happen, Mother Miriam came over to me and hugged me. It was clear she wanted to share her grief with me. Her eyes were moist.

She said to me, "Jesus said someone is going to betray him and that his death is imminent. I cannot bear those words." Her voice reflected deep anguish though her face remained serene. I tried to comfort her.

We stayed in the house for the night. The next morning Jesus said to us, "You are the chosen ones! Come with me." He then left the house and started walking to the temple. The rest of us followed.

Jesus, accompanied by his disciples, moved inside the beautifully decorated porch in front of the temple. Other rabbis from different parts of the country were there, explaining the significance of several things to their followers. The authorities had given all rabbis the right to talk to their disciples there.

When Jesus started to talk about God's kingdom, many Sadducees who were members of the priesthood and the elders arrived, bringing with them an aura of authority.

It was unusual for members of the priesthood to come to hear the advice of a rabbi from Galilee. It soon became clear their real intention wasn't to learn about God's kingdom, but to provoke Jesus. They were visibly angry.

One of the priests came forward and asked Jesus, "Who gave you the authority to advise the public?" Though Jesus was talking to his disciples, the priests had heard that he preached to the general public as well.

"Let me also ask you all one thing," Jesus replied. "If you give me the correct answer, I will answer your question."

The Sadducees agreed.

"From where did John get his baptism: from heaven or from people?"

I thought about this. If the priests answered "from heaven," I knew Jesus would ask them why they didn't believe him. If they answered "from people," it would appear as if the priests were holding people in awe which is very uncomfortable for them.

The priests appeared confused. They looked at each other. "We do not know," they finally murmured.

"Then I am not saying who gave me the authority to preach here either," Jesus said firmly. "I will ask you one more thing. Once there was a man who had two sons. He went to the older one and said, 'Son, go and work in the vineyard today.' The son answered that he didn't want to. But later he changed his mind and went. The father also went to the other son and said the same thing. This son answered, 'Yes, sir,' but didn't go. Which one of the two did what the father wanted?"

"The older one," the priests answered.

Jesus said to them, "I tell you, the tax collectors and the prostitutes are going to the kingdom of God ahead of you. That is the truth. For John the Baptist came to you, showing you the right path to take, and you wouldn't believe him. But the tax collectors and prostitutes believed him and attained salvation. Even when you knew this, you didn't change your minds and believe him."

The priests and the elders didn't have anything to say. They bowed their heads and departed.

During that visit, Jesus left the traders alone but reprimanded the Pharisees and their chief priests in ample measure.

"How terrible are you, teachers of the Law and Pharisees! You are hypocrites. You slam the door to the kingdom of heaven in people's faces, but you yourself won't go in. Nor do you allow in those who are trying to enter. This is terrible! You snatch away homes from widows yet pray long hours for them. You sail the sea and cross whole countries to win one convert, and when you succeed, you make him twice as deserving of going to hell as you yourselves are! So I tell you, the punishment for all these sins will fall on you this day."

Hearing this, the people became excited. This was the first time someone was openly challenging the Sadducees and the Pharisees.

The onlookers roared in excitement, "Glory be to you, son of David!"

When Jesus felt their excitement might turn violent, he pacified the crowd.

That night, Jesus went to a lonely place—Gethsemane, where there was a beautiful garden—to pray and spend the night. Peter and Peter's brother Andrew went along. They stayed in the remains of a structure housing a pressing machine used to squeeze oil from olives. The disciples placed a blanket on the slightly raised platform, and Jesus sat on it, with his disciples on the floor in front of him.

There was faint moonlight during the first hours of the night. Jesus began to talk in a voice filled with grief, saying, "The sorrow in my heart is so great it's crushing me. Stay here and keep watch with me."

Then he bent down on his knees, and prayed, "My Father, if it's possible, take this cup of suffering from me. Yet do not what I want, but what you want."

Some of the disciples fell asleep, as they were very tired. I also needed sleep. When Jesus realized Peter and Andrew were sleeping, he woke Peter and questioned him. "How is it that you two were not able to keep watch with me for even an hour?" Hearing this, everybody woke up.

Jesus told his disciples, "The hour has come for the Son of Man to be handed over to the power of sinful men." In an utterly calm tone, he instructed, "Look! Here is the man who is going to betray me."

The disciples turned their gaze in the direction Jesus was indicating with his hand. They saw Judas arriving. Along with him was a large crowd armed with swords and clubs. A dozen or so soldiers of Antipas, carrying cressets and wearing swords under their belts, were right behind the crowd.

As soon as we saw the crowd approach, Mother Miriam, Joann, and I ducked behind the olive-pressing machine in an effort to conceal ourselves. I watched from the corner of the machine as Judas went straight to Jesus and greeted him. "May peace be with you, Master!" As he was saying this, he kissed the prophet's hand.

As Jesus began asking Judas what this was all about, a soldier came up to Jesus and grabbed him tight to arrest him. Among the crowd were some onlookers who were not in the plot to detain Jesus, and a few were his followers. One drew his sword and struck at the soldier, cutting off his left ear.

Jesus admonished the man, saying, "Put your sword back in its place! All those who take the sword will die by the sword. Don't you know I could call on my Father in heaven for help, and at once he would send me more than twelve armies of angels? But in that case, how could the scriptures come true, which say that this is what must happen?"

Turning to the crowd, Jesus asked, "Why did you come with swords and clubs to capture me, as though I am an outlaw? Every day I sat down and taught in the temple, and you didn't arrest me. To fulfill what the prophets said, it must happen this way."

Terrified by how Jesus was being treated, all the disciples ran away.

Watching the events unfold, Mother Miriam, Joann, and I were also terrified, but we kept hiding until the soldiers departed.

***

We later found out that those who detained Jesus had taken him to the residence of Caiaphas, the high priest of Jerusalem, where the teachers of the law and the elders had already gathered secretly as a council to conduct a trial.

As Jesus was being led away, Peter alone followed them from a distance. He went as far as the courtyard of the high priest's house and sat down there in a corner with guards all around him.

Later he told Jesus's followers what happened. The council began to look for false witnesses against Jesus, so they could build a case and crucify him as a punishment. Several people said many things, but no clear evidence of a crime against the kingdom or state on Jesus's part emerged.

Finally, two men—who we were to find out later had accepted two silver coins each from the priests as a bribe to bear false witness—stepped forward and said, "This man said, 'I am able to tear down God's temple and three days later build it back up!'"

Jesus remained quiet. The high priest, Caiaphas, stood up and asked him, "Why are you not saying anything?"

Jesus still kept quiet.

"Tell us if you are the messiah, the son of God," Caiaphas impatiently demanded.

"Yes, I am," Jesus replied in a firm voice. "From this time on, you will see the son of man sitting at the right side of the Almighty, coming on the clouds of heaven."

Hearing this, the high priest tore his upper garment and shrieked, "Blasphemy!"[3] Then he declared that there was no need for more witnesses, and he asked the council what they thought.

While the trial was going on, a crowd gathered to watch the proceedings.

After a brief meeting, the council declared, "This man is guilty, and he must die!"

Hearing the verdict, the people who were listening became agitated.

---

[3] A ritual Jewish priests do when they hear blasphemy.

Some hit Jesus with their fists, while others spat on his face. One of the high priests approached Peter as he was sitting outside in the courtyard, and said to him, "You too were with Jesus of Galilee!"

Peter outwardly remained calm as he responded, "I do not know what you are talking about." He then went out to the entrance of the courtyard, where he swore three times, "I do not know that man!" Just then, the rooster crowed, and Peter remembered what Jesus had told him. He left the courtyard and began to weep bitterly.

***

Although the trial council had ordered that Jesus be hanged in the morning, they detained him so he might be brought to the palace of Pilate, the Roman procurator. The council was concerned that if the Roman authorities came to know that Jesus, a prophet who had a large following, was sentenced to death on false evidence, they may not approve that decision. So they took Jesus to Pilate to make sure the authorities approved.

***

When Judas found out that Jesus had been sentenced to death, he became distraught. He repented and gave back the thirty pieces of silver to the high priest and the elders, saying, "I have sinned by betraying an innocent man, and he has been sentenced to death."

They replied, "What do we care about that? That is your business."

Judas threw the coins to the floor and left, despondent.

The next day at sunset, a passerby discovered the lifeless body of Judas hanging on a cypress tree branch, not far from the temple.

Shortly thereafter, Caiaphas and his men brought Jesus in front of Pontius Pilate for an audience. "Are you the king of Jews?" Pilate asked Jesus.

"So you say," Jesus replied.

Jesus also said nothing in response to the accusations the high priests and elders there hurled at him. So Pilate asked him, "Don't you hear all these things they are accusing you of?"

Jesus refused to speak a single word. This greatly surprised Pilate, who wasn't fully convinced of Jesus's guilt. He knew the Jewish authorities handed Jesus over to him because they were jealous of the prophet.

During Passover, the custom of the Roman procurator was to set free a prisoner that the public asked for. The Romans called this tradition "administrative mercy." Along with Jesus, there was a well-known prisoner, Barabbas, in custody for murdering a Roman soldier. So when a crowd gathered, Pilate asked, "Which one do you want me to set free for you? Barabbas or Jesus called Messiah?"

"Barabbas, Barabbas!" the crowd chanted at the urgings of the priesthood.

"What shall I do with Jesus called Messiah?" Pilate asked the crowd.

"Crucify him!" the assembled people answered.

Hearing this, Pilate asked a maid to bring him some water in a basin and a washcloth. Washing his hands in front of the crowd, he declared, "I am not responsible for the death of this man! This is your doing." He then ordered Barabbas's release. And he ordered Jesus to be whipped before being handed over for crucifixion.

Pilate's soldiers took Jesus into the governor's palace. They stripped off his clothes and put a scarlet robe on him. Then they made a crown out of thorns and placed it on his head. They hit him and mocked him, saying, "Long live the king of Jews!"

Then the soldiers took the robe off and put Jesus's own clothes back on him, which was the normal procedure of the Roman authorities before crucifying someone.

The soldiers took Jesus to a place called Golgotha, meaning the Place of Skull. They offered Jesus wine mixed with a bitter herb; but after a taste, he refused to drink it.

They then crucified Jesus and divided his clothes among them. After that they sat there, watching as he hung on the cross.

At noon, the whole country became covered with darkness, which lasted for several hours. Around three in the afternoon, Jesus cried out, "My God, my God, why did you abandon me?"

After a few more seconds, he breathed his last.

Suddenly the earth shook! The curtain hanging in the sanctum of the temple was torn in two; rocks were split apart; and graves broke open.

When the sergeant and his soldiers who were guarding Jesus saw these ill omens, they were terrified. Screaming, "He really was the son of God!" they ran away.

These events I watched with Joann and Mary, the mother of disciples James and Joseph, from a distance.

***

That evening, a wealthy follower of Jesus named Joseph went to Pilate and asked for the body of Jesus. Pilate gave orders for the body to be given to Joseph.

Joseph wrapped the body in new linen and placed Jesus in his own tomb, which he had just recently had dug out of solid rock. He had his servants roll a large stone across the entrance to the tomb to keep everyone out.

The other women and I watched over the tomb all night.

The next day, which was the Sabbath, the high priests and the Pharisees went to Pilate's palace and made this request: "Sir, we remember that while that liar Jesus was alive, he was saying, 'I will be raised to life three days later.' So please give orders for his tomb to be carefully guarded until the third day. This will prevent his disciples from stealing his body and then telling the people that he was raised from death."

Pilate granted their wish and made the tomb secure by putting a seal on the stone and leaving one of his own guards on watch.

After the Sabbath day had passed, the other Mary and I went to Jesus's tomb. Suddenly there was a violent earthquake. An angel of the Lord came down from heaven, rolled the mammoth stone away, and perched on it. His appearance was like lightning; his clothes were as white as snow. The guards ran away, they were so afraid of this angel.

The angel spoke to us women: "You must not be afraid. The crucified Jesus is no longer here. He has risen, just as he said. Come here and see the place where he was lying. Go quickly *now*, and tell the disciples he has been raised from death."

Saying this, the angel disappeared into the clouds. We went into the tomb to see for ourselves that Jesus wasn't there. The white shroud that covered his body was there, but not his lifeless body. Although we were afraid, we were also happy in knowing that Jesus had risen. We left the tomb in a hurry to tell the disciples the good news.

On our way to find the other disciples, Jesus suddenly met us and said with a smile, "Peace be with you!"

He reassured us too: "No one should be afraid! Now, go and tell my brothers to go to Galilee and that there they will see me."

Jesus then disappeared into the clouds.

We did as Jesus asked. The eleven disciples went to the hill in Galilee, where Jesus had told them to go. They saw him there, and so they worshipped him, although some doubted that he was the real Jesus.

Jesus came closer to them and said, "I have been given all authority in heaven and on earth! Go then to tell all people everywhere, and make them my disciples! Baptize them in the name of the Father, the Son, and the Holy Spirit, and teach them to obey my commandment. I will be with you always, to the end of the ages."

Saying this, Jesus blessed all the disciples. He then told us he wanted to meditate and slowly walked away from us.

CHAPTER 10

After Jesus's resurrection, I was so despondent that I spent several days in the house without doing anything. My mind was empty, and Alka commented—half in jest and half in seriousness—that her only wish was that she die after seeing me restored to good spirits. But I remained uninterested in everything.

After a while, I decided it wasn't right to remain cloistered like that; I knew I should prepare myself for any sacrifice and I should be spreading the messages of Jesus among the people.

***

Around that time, a relative of mine from the town of Asya visited Magdala on business, and he paid me a visit too. We talked about many things. Then he suggested I visit Asya and spend some time there. It was his opinion that I would find many opportunities there to spread God's message and to do my missionary work.

So when the spring came, I acted on my relative's suggestion: I left for Asya with Sabed and Alka. By then, Sabed had become a follower of Jesus and had sold our business with my consent. Three or four believers also followed us.

Asya was a midsize town, and my disciples and I decided to live in a small village on the outskirts of Asya. I didn't wish to live in the middle of the town, as it was too crowded with people of every type.

We selected a villa perched on a hill on the eastern side of the village. There was a beautiful garden attached to this villa; in fact, the garden was the reason we decided on that house. Also, when we stood on the hill, we could enjoy stupendous views of the valley below.

There also was a walking path bordering the villa, which led to an arbor from which we could see rows of majestic cypress trees, which descended the hillside and extended across the valley. The path was nearly a mile long, and I sometimes took my morning walks along it.

The plan we developed to spread the gospel with my relative was simple. In the beginning, Sabed and Gayose—a young man who had accompanied us from Magdala—would go to a spot in the town where people had gathered. It might be a marketplace or an administrative center. Then they would shout at the top of their voices, "The arrival of the kingdom of God is imminent. You should hear God's message!"

If people heard these words, they were likely to ask more questions out of mere curiosity. At that point, Sabed and Gayose would take them to a quiet place and try to explain to them the greatness of Jesus in simple terms. If they remained interested in what we had to say for a week or so, we would invite them to visit our house for fellowship.

In due course, our group was on a firm footing. Our discussion group had started with five or six people; after three or four months, we had attracted nearly a hundred. In the beginning, we had conversations and study sessions in the villa itself. As our numbers grew, we shifted the sessions to the large, flat expanse on the southern side of the villa. For this we constructed a large tent with a decorated canopy to provide shelter during inclement weather.

When I talked to the group, I tried to explain Jesus's parables to them. Most of them didn't understand much of what I said, but I didn't let that discourage me. I repeated God's message many times, using examples from their own lives. At times, this took the form of question-and-answer sessions that lasted for hours. As a group, we met twice a week.

One day I found out that some ignorant people in our own group were spreading false information about the kingdom of God. Obviously, they were not yet free from the embrace of Satan.

I separated these individuals from the rest of the group and entrusted Sabed with the responsibility of overseeing their studies. Some of them even lacked the necessary discipline to sit quietly for an hour to listen attentively, but Sabed was adept at handling such people. However, the majority of people would listen to my talk of Jesus's message with fervor and humility.

***

A number of Jews who pretended to have spiritual powers themselves came to know about our group. These seven men were all sons of a Jewish priest named Sceva.

They usually traveled around the town and drove out evil spirits. While practicing this sorcery, they claimed they also had the healing power of Jesus. But their main goal was to exploit poor people and make money for themselves.

I came to know about all this from Sabed. "Do ordinary people believe in them?" I asked him.

"Yes! Most of the common folks are gullible; they do not have the ability to distinguish between good and bad. What Sceva and his sons are doing is shameful. They promise the people they will cure their illness if they give sacrificial goats or hens to Sceva. These cheats demand money from the poor people for their service and tell the people they will reach heaven by handing the money over," Sabed answered in disgust.

"What can we do in this matter?" I asked anxiously.

Sabed only said, "Let me try."

After two or three days, Sabed told me Sceva's seven sons had retreated from Asya.

Sabed had in his study group a student who was a sergeant in the Roman army. Sabed mentioned briefly to this student about Sceva's sons and the fraudulent activities they were conducting in Jesus's name.

The sergeant decided to confront them directly. This happened when the brothers were assembled in the main square of Asya, as usual. They had a thurible in front of them, and they started singing songs and playing an instrument resembling an accordion. To receive their blessings, a few people were gathered around them, with chickens as their offering. One had a small lamb with him.

The Roman sergeant arrived with three soldiers to confront the imposters. He cut straight through the crowd and approached one brother, asking of him in an authoritative tone, "Why are you dragging Jesus's name into your witchcraft?"

"Who are you to ask this question? Don't you know we are religious preachers?" the eldest of the brothers haughtily replied.

Before he had stopped talking, the sergeant gave him a heavy blow on his right cheek. Another brother came up to block the blow, but it was in vain, and one of the soldiers broke the brother's leg with his spear. All seven sons of Sceva ran away from the square. They never dared assemble there again to carry on their deceptive trade.

All the Jews and Gentiles in Asya heard about Sceva's story. At first, they were fearful, but later they all sang praise to the Lord.

There were others in Asya who made money practicing sorcery. When they heard about the plight of Sceva, they were scared. They brought their books dealing with sorcery to the main square and burned them in front of the public. Someone added up the price of the books burned, and the total came to five thousand silver coins. In this powerful way, the word of the Lord spread all over Asya.

***

Another conflict took place there during that time. Its root cause was our group spreading the message of Jesus among ordinary people.

I mentioned earlier that Asya was a town populated by people from different lands. The majority of them were Ephesians. They worshipped idols, and their goddess was Artemis, for whom they had built a large temple in the center of the town. The copper walls inside the temple were decorated with figurines of Artemis made of silver. Ordinary folks gave these to the temple as offerings to please their favorite goddess.

Yet the public wasn't allowed inside the temple. Every day, in the morning and evening, the priests assembled at the temple's main gate to accept the offerings of the public. Depending on the value of the offerings, they gave the devotees something in return; most often, it was a slice of bread or a flower.

The Ephesians arrived daily to worship the goddess Artemis. They wanted their deity to solve different problems for them. They asked that their children's diseases be cured, that the family breadwinner's job be protected, and that their daughters be able to find suitable grooms. These were the kinds of requests they made.

The main offering the common people made to the goddess Artemis was her figure made of silver. At some point in their lifetime, every Ephesian needed to offer one silver statue to the temple. Depending on the devotee's financial status, the size of the figure was small or large.

This practice had a commercial side to it: when there wasn't enough space on the interior copper walls to hang these statues, the temple's head priest would sell them. He then would share the proceeds from this illicit trade with his fellow priests.

This monetary transaction was conducted in extreme secrecy. The Ephesians believed all their offerings were used to decorate the temple walls—and that's why the priests didn't allow the public to enter the inner sanctum of the temple.

Demetrius, a prosperous silversmith in town, helped the head priest conduct the secret sale of Artemi statues. In this way, he made a good profit and was able to employ a large number of workers in his shop to make the statues.

When more and more people showed interest in listening to my talk and wanted to repent, Demetrius worried that this would adversely affect his illicit trade. To remove people's faith in pagan traditions, I was emphasizing in my speeches that man-made idols are not gods and have no divine quality. This made Demetrius very angry. If, after listening to my speech, the Ephesians stopped buying and offering figures to the temple, it jeopardized his business.

Therefore, Demetrius decided I needed to be silenced. With his friends, he started a riot in the city. One Friday, a hundred or so of his workers assembled in the city's main square. They were all Ephesians and were shouting many things. They stomped their feet with raised hands, as if they were dancing, but all were agitated. Demetrius was in the front, leading the rowdy crowd.

By evening, more of Demetrius's workers from his various shops had arrived. Standing on a raised platform built for the event, Demetrius made a short speech: "A lady from the faraway Magdala has come to our city and is spreading all sorts of false rumors about the gods! If the Ephesians do not stop this, Artemis's name may come to mean nothing, and the temple and her greatness will be destroyed. Then there is the danger that our business also may disappear."

These words whipped the crowd into a frenzy. The people became furious and started shouting, "Great is the Artemis of Ephesus!" This uproar spread its way throughout the city.

A few of Demetrius's younger workers began to snatch sacred garlands and bags of rice and barley away from the merchants in the pavement stalls. They also tried to take the merchants' cash boxes by force.

Meanwhile, five or six people tied up Gayose, who had come with me from Magdala, and took him before the unruly crowd. When Sabed, who had gone into the city, saw this, he feared the crowd might harm Gayose and immediately came to inform me of the dangerous events. I didn't know what to do, and I became very worried. Finally, I decided to go to the main square myself to plead with the people gathered there.

After praying to Jesus for his blessings, I got ready to go. At that point, two or three believers rushed up to me, begging me not to go there. One person even prostrated himself before me to block my way.

At the same time, the town's chief, who was a trusted friend of mine, sent a message to me with the same request. So I returned to the villa to try to comfort my distraught followers.

Meanwhile, in the town square, there still was no one giving clear and honest guidance to the angry crowd. Screeching, "Long live Artemis, our goddess!" three or so workers ran with their cressets to a nearby building to attempt to burn it down. But the building they approached was a barrack, built by the Asyan township to house the Roman soldiers stationed in the city.

When the Roman soldiers living there saw enraged people rushing toward them with cressets, they jumped up from their chairs. One cut down the nearest worker in front of him with his sword.

Realizing things were moving beyond his control, Demetrius ran to the house of the town chief. The chief, a wise old man respected by many for his tact and forbearance, immediately proceeded to the town square. Upon arrival, he requested that the people there be peaceful.

At first, the chief's entreaties were not received with much favor. However, the sound of a horn from the Roman barracks and the sight of a contingent of twenty or thirty soldiers marching toward them effectively subdued the crowd.

"Our town will safeguard the temple of Artemis until the end of the world. We will protect her greatness at any cost," the chief promised as he addressed the crowd. "You brought Gayose here in captivity, trying to humiliate him. But he is not a person who plunders the temple or speaks ill of the goddess! If Demetrius and his workers have any grievances, there are procedures to address them. Let them appear before the town justice council. If there are other issues, they should petition the charity board. If Demetrius incites our people to violence rather than following established procedures, there is a reasonable chance the Romans will indict us. So I want everyone to go home."

As the crowd dispersed, the town chief set Gayose free as well and sent him to see me.

After this incident, I chose not to stay in Asya for long. When the time came for me to leave for Magdala, all the disciples assembled in our tent for one final prayer. Addressing them, I said, "Since the first day I came to Asya, each one of you has shown me great kindness. You all know the sufferings I have endured because of the enmity of the Jewish priesthood. However, in God's name, I have forgiven them.

"I am extremely happy to note that you have repented and accepted Jesus as your Savior. I have not shielded from you any of God's commandments. Now, please let me go. Let God be with you!"

Saying this, I bent down and prayed with them. I noticed the eyes of all those present were misty.

I had difficulty controlling my emotions as well.

CHAPTER 11

Of all the people Jesus had selected to spread his message, Peter was the one who traveled continuously to do it. His energy and enthusiasm were amazing. The discourses he gave in Galilee, Samaria, and Judea after Jesus's crucifixion increased peoples' understanding of God's kingdom, making them realize the importance of repentance and encouraging them to follow Jesus's commandments in their daily lives.

I traveled with Sabed in Magdala and in the nearby villages to talk to people about the kingdom of God. But in those early days, we followers of Jesus didn't coordinate our activities. When we arrived at a village, five or six people interested in the gospel would show up to hear us. Sometimes there would be none. There was a reason for this: Judea was still under the control of the Romans, who had made it known that if anyone even mentioned the name of Jesus or talked about the gospel, they would be subjected to severe punishment. So only the very devoted—those who were willing to give up their lives—dared to associate with us.

Favorable circumstances for our ministry often arose when a person was cured of a disease by our prayer or when someone saw our suffering because of our devotion to Jesus.

***

One day Sabed told me that Peter and his followers were going to Yoppa the next day. Yoppa was a small village some distance from Magdala. Normally, Peter wasn't much interested in letting woman participate in missionary work. So I didn't know why he told Sabed it would be good if I accompanied him to Yoppa.

I accepted this invitation from Peter. Sabed would be going as well.

The next day, when Peter saw me, he seemed pleased. "Mary, you should join me!" he said affectionately.

"I would be glad to. We are all obligated to spread the greatness of Jesus!" I responded.

"Yes! But I think you are concerned that women are not given sufficient importance in our ministry." He cast a doubtful glance at me.

"That is true. But this is not my feeling alone. Most women in Jerusalem and Nazareth share it with me." Here I stopped short. And although Peter didn't respond to my comment, I felt he got the point.

In Jewish custom, women are excluded from performing certain religious functions (*mitzvoth*). They are also separated from men during prayer by a curtain. The combination of these two practices led to the belief among women in Jerusalem and the neighboring towns that women are inferior to men. We suspected that Peter wanted to perpetrate these customs in our newly formed ministry also.

Then Peter briefly explained to me the reason for his journey to Yoppa. Apparently, in Yoppa, he had a disciple named Tabitha. She had been born to a prosperous family and throughout her life had performed numerous deeds of kindness and charity. Tabitha had fallen sick and died. Her family had washed her body and laid it in an upper bedroom. Peter felt it was his obligation to comfort the parents of Tabitha, as it was the practice of Jesus's followers in their work to comfort the sick and their loved ones.

I was happy Peter invited me on this mission, and I said thanks to God.

We arrived in Yoppa at noon the next day. Unlike the streets of many Judean villages, Yoppa's were wide and clean. On both sides of the street were beautiful plants with many flowers. The people there were well dressed, and they were quite friendly to us.

After making several inquiries, we proceeded on to the home of Tabitha's family. Her father came out to receive us, grief at his daughter's passing evident on his face. Since it was time for lunch, he invited us to have something to eat. Peter said he would do it later and asked as to Tabitha's body.

We were ushered into an upstairs bedroom, where the body of Tabitha lay on a large bed. Her eyes were closed, and it was apparent life has gone out of her thin body.

Tabitha's room was decorated with many-colored cloths. Looking at her body, I concluded she was close to thirty years of age.

A number of women were standing in the room weeping. They showed us all the beautiful garments and tunics Tabitha had made. Then Peter sent them all out of the room. He knelt and prayed. Turning to the body in the bed, he directed, "Tabitha, arise!"

She slowly opened her eyes. When she saw Peter, she tried to sit up, and she gave us a faint smile. Since she didn't have the strength, Peter gave her his hand and raised her up. Then he called back the saints and presented her alive to her family.

Tabitha's father and the others who came to the room were ecstatic; everyone sang God's praises. As I saw this event unfold, my eyes welled up with tears of joy. I too said praise to God many times for his kindness.

The confidence in Jesus of those assembled there increased even more. "Glory be to you Jesus, son of David," we chanted repeatedly.

Peter accepted the invitation of Tabitha's grateful father to have lunch in Tabitha's house.

After resting for a while, I decided to return to Magdala in the evening. But Peter wanted to stay in Yoppa for a few more days. In a nearby village called Tolkotta, Peter had a relative named Simon. Simon insisted that Peter spend time with him. Peter wanted to oblige Simon, whom he hadn't seen for many years.

Sabed told me he wanted to stay with Peter a while longer. I knew Peter loved Sabed like a son, especially since he didn't have one of his own. So I granted Sabed's wish.

The story Sabed told me after his return added to the glory of Jesus. So I shall narrate it here briefly.

Kaiserya is a large district that included Yoppa, Tolkotta, and a few other adjoining villages. Its administrative center was Ithalika, a midsize town. Cornelius was a regimental commander in King Antipas's army; he was based in Ithalika.

Cornelius was a pious man; he and his family worshipped God. He also did much to help the Jewish poor. Unlike other military chieftains, he wasn't cruel and was charitably disposed. He was never satisfied unless he fed three or four impoverished people a day.

Cornelius's custom was to pray twice daily: once in the morning and once in the evening. One morning while praying, he had a vision in which he clearly saw an angel of God coming down in the form of a stout young man. He wore a white cloak and a gold headband.

When Cornelius tried to raise his head to look at the youth, the angel forbade him with a motion of his right hand. The angel then told Cornelius to continue to pray. So Cornelius did. While he was immersed in prayer, the youth told him, "God is pleased with your prayers and works of charity. So he is ready to answer you. Send two men now to Yoppa to bring to you a certain religious man named Peter." The angel then disappeared.

As soon as Cornelius heard this command, he explained his vision to his faithful military guard and one of his assistants and sent them to Yoppa to fetch Peter.

When Cornelius's people arrived in Yoppa, Peter was sitting in the verandah of the house in which he was living, and thinking about an incident that had taken place in the morning. During his morning prayer, he had heard a voice that said, "Do not consider anything unclean that God has declared clean." This was said three times.

Peter conversed with the people Cornelius had sent. When he understood their mission, he agreed to accompany them to Ithalika. He thought there was a connection between the voice he'd heard that morning and the message brought to him by Cornelius's men. Three or four believers who had repented also went with Peter.

He later confided in me the details about his visit to Ithalika. As Peter journeyed to Ithalika, he was burdened by thoughts: *It must be God's will that I go. Otherwise what use would a just and pious Jew who is also a military chief have for me, an ordinary citizen and a humble follower of Jesus? How did this dignitary come to know about me? Is there perhaps a hidden agenda behind this man's invitation as well?*

When Peter met Cornelius in person, he realized all his worries were nonsense. For as soon as he reached the door of Cornelius's house, Cornelius came forward and prostrated himself in front of Peter. This was an unusual honor indeed. Jews would prostate only before God, and never before a man, as this went against their religious beliefs.

"Sir, please get up! I am myself only a man!" Peter reassured Cornelius.

Cornelius did as he was instructed, and both men went into the house. In the interior was a large courtyard where twenty or twenty-five people were already waiting. These were Cornelius's relatives and friends, whom he had invited over to hear Peter.

Seeing so many people present startled Peter at first, and he whispered to Cornelius in a hushed voice, "You know very well that a Jew is not allowed by his religion to associate with Gentiles. But our God says that I must not consider any person ritually unclean or defiled. That is why I came over when you sent for me."

Cornelius replied, "You are God's messenger! I sent for you because of the command I received during my prayer."

"What was that command?" Peter asked.

"I was first told that God has heard my prayers and taken notice of my works of charity. The command said that for me to get God's protection, I should send someone to Yoppa to get Peter, who was residing there with a tanner named Simon, and listen to his testimony. These people I invited are very eager to listen to your testimonial."

When Peter heard these words, he became ecstatic. It was incredible to have a high official—and a military man with considerable authority—invite a disciple of Jesus to his home not so long after a trial had ordered the prophet crucified and also declared that the saying of Jesus's name would invite severe punishment. Moreover, that high official had shown Peter great respect by prostrating before him, and he was eagerly awaiting Peter's testimony. This was a man wanting to repent.

Peter went down the steps into the courtyard, where he prayed for a few seconds. Then slowly but firmly he addressed the assembled guests. "I now realize that it's true that God treats everyone on the same basis. Whoever fears him and does what is right is acceptable to him, no matter what race he belongs to. You know the message he sent to the people of Israel, proclaiming the good news of peace through Jesus Christ, who is Lord of all. You know of the great event that took place throughout the land of Israel, which began in Galilee after John preached his message of baptism. You know of Jesus of Nazareth and of how God poured out on him the Holy Spirit and power.

"Jesus went everywhere, doing good and healing all who were under the power of the devil, for God was with him. We are witnesses of everything that he did in the land of Israel and in Jerusalem. Then they put him to death by nailing him on a cross. But God raised him from death three days later; He caused him to appear, not to everyone, but only to those witnesses whom God had already chosen—that is, to us, those who ate and drank with him after he rose from death.

"And he commanded us to preach the gospel to the people and to testify that he is the one whom God has appointed as the judge of the living and the dead. All the prophets spoke about him, saying that everyone who believes in him will have his sins forgiven through the power of his name. Let you all be blessed!"

Everyone present went up to Peter and welcomed him wholeheartedly. They believed his testimony.

Watching all this, the believers who had come with Peter from Yoppa also were amazed. They all sang praise to the Lord many times.

After saying praise to the Lord one more time, Peter made arrangements with Cornelius to baptize those who were present, after which he returned to Yoppa.

When Sabed came back to Magdala, he vividly narrated this event to me. I was overjoyed and praised him.

CHAPTER 12

In an earlier chapter, I wrote about some of the travels I took with Peter to different villages to spread the gospel. When the political circumstances in Jerusalem changed, it became exceedingly difficult to continue this practice.

The authorities came to view our missionary work as subversive, so they suppressed it with all the tools available to them. It made them angry even to hear people saying the name of Jesus. They considered any gathering of five or six Jewish people to be a threat.

Even under such circumstances, the disciples relentlessly strove to help the needy and spread Jesus's message among the people in Jerusalem and the surrounding areas. These activities formed the nucleus of the early Christian church.

Peter and I used to go daily to the temple in Jerusalem for prayer, where I rented a house to stay. I had no problem doing so; I had always respected Moses's commandments; I had believed in them from my early childhood. It was only the misinterpretation of those laws by the priesthood that I detested.

One day, when Peter was returning from his prayer, he spotted a disabled beggar at the outer door of the temple. The man appeared to be around fifty years of age, but both his legs were so small they looked like those of a five- or six-year-old child. He was very skinny, and his face was full of grief. His right hand didn't have a palm. He was a beggar who deserved all kindness.

Peter looked at the man's face for a few seconds intently. Then he touched the beggar's arm and said, "To you I do not have silver or gold coin to give. I am asking in the name of Jesus that strength be returned to your legs and body so that you will be able to work."

A miracle happened right then. Suddenly, the man's body and his legs grew strong. The beggar got up and slowly walked forward. Saying praises to Jesus, he walked down the steps of the temple and disappeared into the crowd.

Many people soon heard about this miraculous event. They gathered around Peter and John, who in turn talked to them about the Holy Ghost and the resurrection of Jesus.

Naturally, the temple authorities also heard about it. One day, on their orders, the security officials handcuffed both disciples and sent them to prison for the night.

The next day, Peter and John were brought before the justice council. Luckily, they didn't have to face the fate of Jesus. After a trial, they were freed with only a warning. However, Caiaphas threatened both of them at one point and in a grave manner told them not to undertake further missionary work in the name of Jesus.

***

From early on, I hated both Caiaphas and his father-in-law, Anas. They were sinister in their dealings with other members of the priesthood who wanted to make the administration of the temple transparent. Caiaphas was interested only in amassing wealth for himself and his cronies. After Jesus's crucifixion, my anger toward him became so intense, I would not have hesitated to pierce his heart with a dagger, if such an opportunity arose.

But as I thought on Jesus's words, I calmed down. It was he who had said, "Those who take to the sword will be destroyed by the sword." The vengeance in me slowly disappeared.

Then I began to feel sympathy toward both men. What ignorant human beings they were! "Let God be merciful to them," I prayed.

None of the disciples allowed threats or cruel treatment to discourage them. Nor did I. We continued the missionary work with vigor.

One time, Caiaphas and his men arrested many disciples of Jesus— including me—and sent us to a public prison. Life there was indeed a new experience to me. We spent time with ordinary criminals in a narrow and dark room. At first I was afraid, and then I felt sympathy for them.

The next day, we were taken before the justice council. Caiaphas and Anas presided over the council, right beside several leading members of the priesthood. When I saw them, hatred slowly raised its ugly head again within me, but I kept silent.

Caiaphas came forward and said in a loud voice, "The council has given to all of you strict orders not to teach in his [Jesus's] name. But see what you have done!"

Peter answered, "We must obey God, and not men. The God of our ancestors raised Jesus from death, after you killed him by nailing him to the cross. The Savior gave the people of Israel the opportunity to repent and have their sins forgiven. We are witnesses to these events. Whatever are God's commands—that is what we will follow."

Without hiding my fury, I asked, "We are fulfilling the orders of the God in heaven, so why should we follow men's orders?!"

When Caiaphas and his council heard this, they were so enraged they decided to have the apostles put to death. The bloodthirsty council's verdict shocked all present in the audience.

At that moment, a Pharisee named Gamaliel, who was a highly respected teacher of Moses's law stood up in the council and said, "Fellow Israelites, be careful what you do to these men and woman. Leave them alone! If what they have planned and done is of human origin, it will disappear; but if it comes from God, you cannot possibly defeat them. You could find yourself fighting against God."

When Caiaphas heard this, he knew the common people would value Gamaliel's opinion, for the man was a respected scholar of the laws of Moses.

So Caiaphas stared ahead quietly for a few seconds then softened his position. He requested the council at least punish the disciples for disturbing the peace in a public square. The other council members agreed to this and ordered the disciples and me to be whipped ten times in public.

The officer in charge of the temple's security dragged us to a private prison and whipped us each ten times. This experience was demeaning and painful. The beating from the guard's whip left blue lines all over my body, and in some areas my skin was lacerated, and there was blood.

However, none of us wept as we were disgraced in this way. The belief that we were following God's commandments gave us the strength to bear the pain and humiliation.

While we were being set free, the security guards again gave us strict orders not to preach in Jesus's name.

***

Around that time, the Roman authorities let loose their repressive measures in full force on the believers in Israel. King Antipas had passed away, and his son Agrippa had ascended to the throne. At least Antipas had been diplomatic and had some foresight. Agrippa didn't have these qualities in the least. He would do anything to please the Roman authorities and to protect his kingship. That was his life goal.

After Jesus's departure from our midst, differences of opinion began to surface in our group. (We later began to call it an assembly, due to the increase in the number of believers attending our meetings.) Peter was blunt in his dealings with the disciples, and I found it difficult to agree with his many views.

For example, even when Jesus was alive, Peter had asked me to leave the ministry, as I was a woman. Though he accepted Jesus's messages on all important matters, he clung to his own beliefs in traditional Jewish beliefs and practices. For example, Peter wanted to separate women from men during our prayers on the grounds that it was the practice in synagogues.

I vehemently opposed this idea. I wanted women to be treated as equal to men. Only after Jesus's decisive intervention on my behalf did Peter withdraw his demand. I didn't take personal matters like these seriously, but I did think his ideas about the programs we wanted to pursue in our assembly were dangerous.

Peter was also harsh in his dealings with the disciples who didn't agree with him on matters relating to the new ministry. I remember one incident involving Jacob, who was always thoughtful and tried to help people in need. One day he met a merchant from Syria who was suffering from mental stress. Apparently this merchant had lost a considerable sum of money because his vessels carrying merchandise were lost at sea due to a storm. When he came to our tent, Jacob wanted to comfort him. But

Peter scolded him in front of other disciples and forbade the man any help simply because he was not a Jew.

So Peter and I fought on many occasions about the direction the assembly should take.

Peter was against converting non-Jews into believers. You must understand that the most fundamental belief in Judaism is that Jews are God's "chosen ones." However, Jesus taught us that the children of God are whoever believes in God and that they will be redeemed by the Holy Ghost. So in our early assemblies, a main objective was explaining the contradiction inherent in these two formulations.

Moreover, Jews could only undertake certain prescribed activities on the day of the Sabbath. That was another reason Peter wasn't in favor of taking non-Jews into our assembly.

But non-Jews who didn't believe in our tradition and spoke different languages from us wanted to know more about Jesus's teaching. I argued that there was no point in keeping them away from us. I was always careful to remind my disciples of Jesus's words: everybody is equal before God. But "interested parties" spread rumors that one group of people was getting preferential treatment in the assembly at the expense of another group. Attempts were made to stamp out my group and also Peter's. There was a lot of tension. This made me and other believers feel terrible.

Another topics that emerged in the early days of our assembly was how much importance we should give to the laws of Moses in our new movement. As I indicated before, although Jesus valued Moses's laws and said so often, he gave them a new interpretation. But Jesus's brother James didn't accept this interpretation; he wanted everybody to accept Moses's laws strictly. Being conservative in his religious outlook, he wanted all of us to worship only in the temple and to follow the procedures enshrined in Torah in our everyday life.

Others pleaded that we needed to forget the past and open a new path. But James didn't tolerate their views, and he tried to impose his views on them. Because of such conflicting views, there was much tension within the assembly in Jerusalem.

Yet even Peter, who was always outspoken in expressing his views, didn't oppose James directly. He wanted to give James special consideration due to his being the eldest among us and Jesus's brother.

Ironically, the pretense that James wore the mantel of Jesus is what ultimately took his life away. It's a sad story.

Against the wishes of King Agrippa, James used to preach to the people on religious matters. He talked about extremely emotional topics, such as who the Savior was and when he was coming. Agrippa thought this would cause anxiety among his subjects and create political difficulties for himself. He therefore decided to detain James. The cunning Agrippa mistakenly believed that by harassing Christian believers, he would enhance his prestige among the Jewish people.

It proved easy for Agrippa to imprison James, as he freely moved among his own people. One day, the disciples of Jesus watched with fear and anxiety as Agrippa's soldiers handcuffed James when he was coming out of a synagogue after prayer.

We were terrified at this turn of events, and all the disciples prayed for James. It was in vain. Without even a show of a trial, Agrippa ordered James beheaded. Since it was normal in Israel at the time to crucify ordinary criminals, we believed it was probably because of James's closeness to the priesthood that he was given this dignified death.

Agrippa's soldiers carried out Agrippa's order within his palace courtyard. At the last moment, James faced his executioners while affirming his faith in God.

***

In the early days, the disciples assembled to pray in each other's houses. We never had an actual place for an assembly of our own, as we faced enormous resistance from both the Jewish priesthood and King Agrippa.

The main obstacle in acquiring a plot of our own was that any landowner who sold us the plot had to face the displeasure of the authorities. If someone came forward to sell us a parcel of land, he would be subjected to severe punishment.

Another obstacle to buying a plot was that if we regularly gathered in one place, someone was sure to inform the high priesthood. And Agrippa's spies were all over the place. Since priests had the support of the occupying Roman army, it would be very easy for them to dislodge us from our meeting place. We knew if we violated their orders and met in the same spot thereafter, we would face severe punishment. King Agrippa was trying his very best to persecute us, as he was hoping to curry favor with Pharisees and the Sadducees.

During this time, the high priests humiliated a man named Stephen. He hailed from Greece, and God richly blessed him, so he performed great miracles. But the priesthood detested him for this and had him thrown out of the city without a trial.

The political events prevailing during this time disappointed Peter extremely. With the situation in Jerusalem becoming more dangerous by the day, he finally decided to go to Rome. Some of the other disciples left too—some for Samaria and others for Ethiopia, Cyprus, or Athens.

I decided to leave Jerusalem for Ephesus. Although the Ephesians were nonbelievers, they generally were a loving people, and I had learned their language a bit during my stay in Asya. I sincerely believed that, by living there, I might be able to spread Jesus's message among Ephesians.

***

For a few days, I was confused, not knowing what to do. Then it occurred to me to visit Magdala and live there for about two or three months before going to Ephesus. For the last few years, I had been wandering around after leaving the place of my birth and the house in which I'd spent my early adulthood. I thought visiting the place again may reenergize me.

How can I describe my feelings when I arrived in Magdala? For a long time when I first arrived, I just stood in one spot, looking at the narrow streets paved with cobblestones, the beachhead where the fishermen anchored their boats, and the main marketplace. These all were treasures that time hadn't taken into its hand and played with.

As I moved to walk toward the wharf, I encountered the son of a man who had worked for me as a bookkeeper a long time before. He was taking his boat out of the water after the day's catch.

When this youth saw me, he immediately recognized me. He came up to me and introduced himself. His name was Sylvanis, and he told me he was a believer in Jesus's teachings. He said he had heard about me and my missionary work with Jesus.

Sylvanis requested that I give a sermon on the God's kingdom to the assembly he had organized with a few of his friends right there in Magdala. He told me they met once a week to discuss Jesus's message.

He also invited me to stay with him that night, which I readily accepted. By this time and with my consent, Sabed had sold my house and the family business so that he could become a follower of Jesus.

Sylvanis lived in a one-room flat above a mud house. He prepared his own meals and slept in the same room. He allowed me to sleep on the cot in the room while he slept on the terrace above the house.

The next evening, we went together to the assembly Sylvanis had organized. All those present were very happy to see me. Although they were tired as a result of a day's hard work, mostly in the fields under a hot sun, they exuded resilience and were full of confidence. These common folks wanted to know more about me and the core beliefs underlying Jesus's interpretation of Moses's laws.

"You are one who saw Jesus after his resurrection!" a young man noted with reverence. "So he may have given you a special blessing!"

I replied, "Jesus never showed special preference for anybody. Before him, everybody is equal."

"Still, sister, tell us about everything. We are anxious to hear!" said another attendee. They all affirmed that they wanted to know Jesus's message from someone who had traveled with Jesus and seen him crucified.

I shared with them the message Jesus gave during the last supper, saying, "His commandment was 'Love one another, just as I love you. The greatest love a person can show to his friends is to give his life for them. If you do what I ask you, the Father in heaven will give you whatever you ask of him in my name.'"

I also explained that Jesus talked about the importance of repentance and self-realization. What I meant was that each person has his or her own potential, and through the blessing of the God, he or she can achieve the fulfillment of that potential. I organized my thoughts about these concepts in my mind before answering their many questions. I tried to answer even their minute doubts and questions as best I could. I spent several hours with them.

I also wanted to know something about their assembly: Who had taken the initiative to form it? Had non-Jews also started to believe in

Jesus's teachings? How many people usually attended gatherings? Were the practices any different from those of the Jewish synagogues? How?

After we ate a meal together—the attendees had brought wine and bread—Sylvanis and I returned to his home in the last hours of night.

***

After staying in Magdala for a few weeks, I returned to Jerusalem. Jerusalem! Again, Jerusalem! The political atmosphere there changed every day. Nero, whom many thought was insane, had ascended the throne in Rome. He was a thoroughly immoral man who later committed suicide. Nero sent Galous, his governor in Syria, to suppress the resistance movement in Jerusalem—and provided him with the necessary force to accomplish this.

During the first stage of the war that ensued, the secret warriors of Jewish patriots were able to kill several hundred Roman soldiers, keeping them from entering Jerusalem. For several weeks, they ruled the city, proclaiming, "Praise to the Lord!"

Nero reacted with vengeance: he sent his faithful and very efficient army chief, Vespasian, to conquer Jerusalem. Vespasian had under his command seventy thousand highly trained Roman soldiers, and the plan was to attack Jerusalem from all four sides. This powerful army formation was one that the world had never seen. Vespasian's brutal forces defeated the patriotic Jews after just a few encounters.

His soldiers then searched for every rebellious Jew, and upon finding them, cut them down with their spears. The soldiers robbed the city of its wealth and then burned it as they had Carthage.

Mother Miriam asked that I take her to Nazareth, so one morning, we left for Jerusalem, accompanied by two followers. As we set out, my heart was full of grief. I reflected on my first journey, as a teenager, to the city of Jerusalem: *What remains of the prosperity and glitter I had seen then? Everything is in ruin!* Now I could see only Roman soldiers running around with their cressets to burn the remaining houses or few buildings that stood unscathed.

I remembered what Jesus had prophesied: "This is the end of an age!"

During our journey to Nazareth, Mother Miriam didn't talk much.

She was grief-stricken, although outwardly she showed no sign of it. As usual, she appeared dignified, her face tranquil.

Probably she was gratified in knowing the part her son had played in bringing that age to an end.

After a time, we saw at a distance the hills of Nazareth.

CHAPTER 13

On the day of my departure for Ephesus, I got up very early in the morning. I prayed fervently for Jesus's blessings for the voyage I was about to embark and as I spread his message.

The ship we had arranged to travel on was small; it couldn't carry more than thirty people. It was close to that number already, including me, Sabed, Alka, and our cook, Thaddeus, so we could not carry much luggage. I brought with me only two small boxes containing essential clothing; two or three diaries in which I wrote down my ideas about Jesus's formulation of Moses's teachings; and a hand-drawn picture of Jesus.

Theferios, the captain of our ship, asked that I leave Magdala in the evening and reach the harbor town of Caesarea in the early morning. There was good reason to undertake the journey to Caesarea at night: during the day, Roman soldiers and tax collectors frequented the main path to that town. They would roam around, asking travelers all sorts of questions like, "Where are you going?" and "What are you carrying?" If they thought you had something valuable, they might confiscate it. The captain thought that journeying by night might allow us to avoid those difficulties.

So we left Magdala in the evening and proceeded toward Caesarea on a cart pulled by two donkeys. Around ten at night, we rested for a while in a village west of Aeration. We started out again before sunrise, reaching Caesarea in the morning without encountering either soldiers or tax collectors.

The morning we arrived, the sea was in turmoil because of high winds.

So our captain said it would be better to delay the start of our journey until one following day. So we stayed in Caesarea for the day.

At that time, Caesarea was an important harbor in the Mediterranean Sea. During our brief stay, we saw people in the streets from all different lands and speaking many languages. Most of these were traders: Syrians, who wanted to export their superior-quality swords, shields, and spears; Libyans, who were selling goats' hair; and timber merchants from Hiram. All of them seemed prosperous.

But in one thing I felt sympathy toward them: although these men were rich, the Romans were still exploiting them.

After consulting with the captain, we decided to stay in an inn for the night. We put our belongings in our room, then Alka and I went to the dining area. While we were waiting for our meal, two Roman soldiers walked in and took two seats just across from us. These soldiers, already drunk, talked in loud voices, so we overheard them easily.

"Hey! How much did you get today?" one of them said.

"Nine silvers," the other replied.

"Why? That is not much."

"Did not I mention to you about that merchant from Hiram? I thought of intimidating him to collect some silver today. However, I felt sympathy for him and spared the man. His three barges containing timber were lost at sea because of high winds and hail. Let it be so, my friend. How much did you get?"

"You know that liquor shop just across the street? I extracted twenty silvers from its owner. Recently, he started a brothel business also."

The soldier was surprised. "Oh! Is it so?"

"He has brought in girls of different ages from many lands. To be entertained by one girl, the going rate is four silvers for one hour."

Their conversation went on for a long time, and I was disgusted. These were the officials responsible for the law and order of this town, but they themselves were encouraging graft and crime. I prayed silently to God to shower his wrath on these despicable men.

As it was very late, we finished our meal in a hurry and went to bed.

***

Our ship started on its weeklong voyage the next day. The gentle wind was favorable for sailing, so we headed out and traveled close to the shore.

I didn't interact much with the other passengers, except for two or three of them. One was a Greek man named Aristha Hose. In a short time, we became friends.

For a while, he had been a priest in Greece. At first he had spent his time reading the Greek classics to others and teaching a few people about their mythology. After a few years, he became disinterested in such pursuits. At that time, he heard of Peter and the gospel, and eventually he developed an interest in it. To learn more about Jesus's teachings, Aristha Hose had even visited Jordan.

He was a middle-aged, burly man of medium height. He had a serene face and was humble and soft-spoken. He was also going to Ephesus.

Besides Alka and me, there was one other woman on the ship, Lydia. She was a deeply religious Jew who had never heard about Jesus or his teachings. Whenever she had the time—which was often during our voyage—she would read the Torah. Lydia was older than I by perhaps five or six years.

Marcus was a youth of the same age as Sabed. Energetic and friendly, he was from a Jordanian village. He told us he had listened to the speeches of John the Baptist and had acquired some knowledge about revelation and repentance. He was very interested in the gospels. Once, though, Marcus had talked about these subjects with his friends. King Agrippa's soldiers learned of this and went looking for him. They caught Marcus, tore up his clothes, and plastered his body with mud. Then they subjected him to all sorts of humiliation. Marcus said he had decided to flee the Jordan valley that very day and had been waiting for the opportunity to do so.

He added that he was ready to make any sacrifice to spread Jesus's message among nonbelievers.

***

The first town our ship anchored in was Paphos, Cypress. It took us only two days to reach there. I didn't see any travelers getting down from or entering our ship; I simply saw some men in a small boat bringing jars of pure water and handing them up to the ship's crew. The captain had anchored in Paphos expressly for that purpose.

After leaving Paphos, we traveled for nearly four days without stopping. Since the wind was favorable, the ship sailed west smoothly. The sky was clear. At night, there were shining stars. The full moon spread its glitter everywhere, giving me immense joy.

Only when the captain announced it did we know that the ship had passed the harbor towns of Myrna and Miletus. I had heard about Miletus; it had excellent craftsmen who made clay pots and vases that were well known throughout the Mediterranean for their exquisite beauty and craftsmanship. Miletus was also respected for the quality of its fishing nets.

My aunt Ruth told me once that my late father had many friends there; he had visited it two or three times on business. And in our house, we kept a beautiful vase my father had bought from Miletus as a decorative piece. It was decorated with multicolored pearls and had a silver lining inside it. The vase was such an impressive curio that our neighbors often visited just to see its beauty.

On the fifth day after leaving Paphos, the sky filled with dark clouds, and the sea became turbulent. A strong wind blew southward and violently shook our vessel. Theferios let the ship go south with the flow of wind for a few miles.

In the evening, with much effort, we reached an interior place five or six miles north of Laodicea. There the captain anchored the ship, and we all got out and went onto the beach for our safety.

The question *What will we do next?* was in my mind as it was getting dark.

Theferios gave instructions to the crew to prepare our meal. He then walked around the place for a while with two or three assistants. After making sure there were no wild animals in the vicinity, he decided we should stay there for the night. He also told us that we wouldn't anchor at Sore, another Mediterranean Sea port, in the south, as had been planned. We would go straight on to the seaport town of Tyre in the north.

In the morning, the sky cleared, and the wind subsided. When we were getting ready to leave, I noticed Lydia seemed depressed. She was sitting on the blanket under which she slept at night, simply looking out to the sea. She held the Torah in one hand. She wasn't showing any enthusiasm about getting on board the ship, as the other passengers were.

I placed my hands on her shoulder and prayed with her for a few seconds. Then I asked her earnestly, "Shall we go?"

Lydia wasn't able to speak for a moment; apparently, she was overcome with grief. Then she told her story briefly. Her husband had been a wealthy merchant in Judea; he had died six or seven months ago. Her only son was employed in Sore. She had chosen to set sail with us so that she might go to him. Naturally, when Theferios had announced the ship would no longer anchor at Sore, it was extremely upsetting for her.

A few of us approached Theferios and pleaded with him to anchor the ship at Sore, which is in the south, so Lydia could join her son. But he would not change his mind. He said he could not anchor there for one person; if he did, it would jeopardize the entire journey, as the weather could turn bad again. He explained to us that he had done some meteorological observations about the direction of sea wind and figured out that in a day, the north wind would become favorable to us. Then we would be able to travel quite a distance to the north.

He told Lydia that if she traveled six or seven miles by land from there, she could reach Sore. *But how could she travel through that unfamiliar place alone?* I wondered.

Finally, Theferios said that after the ship reached Tyre, he would make some arrangements for Lydia so she could travel on to Sore. To this she agreed.

As we left the beach, I instructed Alka to give extra care to Lydia.

***

Before reaching Tyre, I talked to Lydia about Jesus's message. At first she didn't show much interest. But after two days of such talk, she wanted to know more.

I was comforted by the thought that Lydia had attained a measure of inner peace listening to stories of the Savior's sacrifice for the human race. As a result of Alka's superb care and my heartfelt and comforting words, Lydia's confidence grew. She now trusted me and agreed to come with us anywhere to do missionary work. She gave up the thought of living with her son.

In Tyre, two or three passengers got out, and just as many got in. The ship stayed there for a short time, just long enough for grain and water to be brought in.

The next day the ship reached Sephardi. Two burly merchants, who had come from Haifa to sell goats' hair, got off. Before his departure, one of the merchants gave a beautiful upper garment made of goat hair to Alka as a present. We didn't stay long in Sephardi—just long enough to anchor and untie the ropes.

From Sephardi, our ship traveled northeast. The wind was favorable. I spent my days stitching sweaters and talking to Lydia about Jesus's messages. Captain Theferios was fond of cooking meals, and on occasion, he brought me some of his delicious preparations. I shared them with Lydia and Aristha Hose. Thaddeus, our cook, aided the captain in his culinary pursuits.

On the seventh evening, we arrived at Ephesus in Asia Minor. The captain threw a piece of lead into the sea and determined the ship was three miles from the shore.[4] Avoiding the rock formations scattered ahead, the captain managed to anchor the ship safely. Only those who belonged to our party and Lydia got down at Ephesus. We thanked the captain and his crew profusely.

We rowed to the shore on a small boat. When we arrived, I was anxious and looked around immediately at this totally new place. I didn't know their language or the character of the country's people. *What sort of reception awaits us?* I wondered. However, I didn't show my feelings.

When we got to the shore, I picked up a handful of soil and kissed it. Then I prayed for the Lord's blessings. Everybody sang hymns.

While we were standing there thinking about what to do next, a young man came toward us. In one hand, he had a big fish, and in the other, a leather bag. On his shoulder was an ax. He walked with measured steps, and his body was slightly bent forward.

At first he was surprised to find us. Then he smiled.

Although the conversation started with sign language, it soon turned into primitive Greek, which Hose knew better than I, and the young man obviously knew.

The young man took us to their village chief, an old man with a long, flowing white beard. At first the chief gave us an inquiring look. Then he

---

4 A method used by ancient seafarers to know the distance from the sea to shore.

talked to the young man in a low voice. After that he asked us to sit down on a mat his assistant had brought to the porch of his house. Although it was built with stones and timber, the small house was well kept.

Hose explained to the village chief where we had come from and what our mission was. The chief didn't seem to show any interest in such things. But I noticed the figure of a female goddess stitched on his turban. The figure was similar to something I had seen somewhere before, but I couldn't recall where.

When the sun was slowly setting, the chief instructed one of his assistants to prepare meals for us. He then extended an invitation for us to stay in his house for the night. We gladly accepted.

CHAPTER 14

The next day, the village chief took us to the area chief. Apparently, an "area" consisted of ten villages, and all village chiefs together elected an area chief.

We found the area chief's quarters close to the village where we stayed when we first arrived from Jerusalem. Only then did we realize that we had two more days of travel before us if we desired to reach Ephesus. We decided to stay in the area for a few days as the chief's guests.

My companions and I stayed in a fairly large village not far from the shore. Although most of the area chief's villages were small, there were two or three fairly large ones as well. Smyrna was a large village, and people called the whole area Smyrna.

People there lived mainly by fishing and hunting. They also farmed wheat and barley, mostly as tenants to big landowners. As among the Galileans, poverty and sickness had wrought havoc there. My desire was to spread Jesus's message among the downtrodden people of Smyrna.

At first, Thenorus, the area chief, viewed us with suspicion. Why he did was obvious: I had seen the image of a woman stitched on his turban, one that resembled the figures of the goddess Artemis I had seen in Asya. It was no wonder a devotee of Artemis viewed us, the messengers of Jesus, with suspicion.

The area chief's house was big and well appointed, as befit his official status. He invited me, Alka, and Lydia to stay with him at his house, and we accepted. The others in our party stayed in another house, which was fairly large also and with all the conveniences.

Since Hose knew the language of the natives, I sent him to different parts of Smyrna to find out more about them. I wanted to know their standard of living, the nature of their worship, and their social structure.

Since most of the people of Smyrna believed in pagan practices, Hose didn't receive a good reception at first. When he tried to interact with people to spread the gospel, they angrily tried to attack him and his assistants.

I still remember a particular incident Hose related to me. One day, he went to the valley of a hill that lay to the north of Smyrna, in the hope of talking to the natives there. Primitives among primitives, the people of that region lived by hunting the rabbits and deer that hopped about on the nearby hill. Since they had no education or mental disciple, they were inclined to attack others on the slightest provocation. There was no formal village structure either—just a few scattered units made in the shape of tents with raw timber. It was very hot that morning, although the sun was still rising in the east.

Hose looked around and spotted the figure of a woman on the top of a big tent. He noticed too, a lad of eleven or twelve eating a half-baked squirrel that hung on a stick he was holding. He wore nothing other than a chain around his waist made of small colored stones hung on a string.

Since the adult men had already left for the hill to go hunting, there were only a few women with bulging bellies and round, reddish eyes. They slowly gathered around Hose and looked at him suspiciously. No one came forward to welcome him.

In the meantime, the boy with the half-baked squirrel disappeared.

"Let the Holy Ghost bless you," Hose slowly said. "I am here to talk to you about the kingdom of God, the coming of which is imminent. Jesus, our Savior, has given his own life to redeem others from their sins—"

When he reached this point, two sharp arrows fell directly in front of him, and he realized that if he persisted in his speech, a third arrow may pierce his head. He made a hasty retreat.

Although this event brought Hose near to death, he didn't give up. In a few months, he was able to lead some important members of that valley to believe in Jesus.

***

Hose was able to continue his ministry in the valley as a result of an unexpected event involving the area chief. Thenorus. It started with Thenorus confiding in me about something that was troubling him deeply: a fear that he might die without a son or daughter. He didn't have any offspring, and he was already sixty years of age. According to that culture's beliefs, it was a sin to have no children. And if a person died without a child, no one related to that person could ascend to the position of area chief. In a society where family ties were so important, Thenorus was concerned that his situation might make him an outcast.

He told me he had commissioned practitioners of witchcraft from different lands to conduct special rituals and prayers so he might produce offspring. But sadly, all those efforts had been in vain. He also continued to have his wife treated by physicians.

As he spoke, I remembered Lydia had been a midwife for several years in her native Judea. So I discussed with her, in strict confidence, the matter that was giving Thenorus so much anxiety and grief. Lydia assured me that she could teach the chief's wife certain exercises she could do while pregnant, in the event that this might be of help to the couple. I also prayed to the Holy Ghost for his blessings on Thenorus and his wife.

Within the year, Thenorus's wife gave birth to a baby boy. Thenorus was overjoyed and publicly announced the news with much pomp and pageantry. He also gave a sumptuous feast to many people to celebrate the auspicious occasion. Knowing that I was Lydia's spiritual leader, Thenorus began to show me even more care and friendship after this happy event. He also told me he was willing to extend assistance to me in my missionary work. And with his assistance, Hose was able to return to the hill valley to resume his work on behalf of Jesus.

Thenorus now was cooperating fully with us on all matters relating to our missionary work.

***

As time passed, the assembly I had organized with Hose's help began to attract more and more people. Many wanted to share their difficulties in life with us; many also wanted to know more about the kingdom of God. So we felt the need for a plot of land with a house of our own.

With Thenorus's help, we obtained a large plot in the center of Smyrna from the town council. Hose and Marcus then visited many wealthy area citizens to raise enough funds to build a hall there for us to pray in.

I decided to erect a cross in the center of the hall, in the hope that this might remind future generation of the sacrifices Jesus made. Hose named the stand on which the cross was placed "the altar." Two Greek sculptors made a large figure of Jesus on the cross in white marble and placed it on the altar with Marcus's help.

We decided to assemble for prayer once a week. In the beginning, we chose to honor God in this way on Thursday. Later we changed the day to Sunday. Since in Ephesus that was a day of rest for the people, we thought Sunday would be a more convenient day for them to meet and pray.

As the number of believers increased, many wanted to know more about spiritual topics. In the beginning, they were hesitant to ask questions in front of others. But Hose and I encouraged them to ask any questions they might have. Slowly there was a positive response.

For example, many wanted to know what I meant when I said, "Live as if God called you." This was a rule I taught every day in our assembly. I explained that all of them should go on living according to the Lord's gift to each of them, and all should remain as they were when they accepted God's call, whatever their social status at the time. I wanted them to believe Jesus was their Savior.

One day after prayer, a short skinny man who was a carpenter stood up and asked, "What are God's commandments?"

Hose replied, "God's commandments are passed on to us through Moses, a great prophet. Anyone who lives not by these commandments is a sinner. He will not reach God's kingdom. Sinners will be judged according to these commandments; those who follow them will be redeemed of their sins by the Holy Ghost, and they will reach God's kingdom. You should remember this."

The carpenter asked, "What did Jesus do for sinners?"

Hose said, "God's love, through the Holy Ghost, has been poured into our hearts. But while we were weak, Jesus sacrificed his own life for our sake. Is there another sacrifice greater than this? God showered on us his love for us through Jesus's death, as he died for our sins."

Hose's rather lengthy explanation seemed to satisfy the carpenter. But since many continued to have questions, we decided to set aside one hour each Sunday for a question-and-answer session. In due course, it became an extremely useful program for everybody. When neither Hose nor I was able to participate in the assembly, we still felt a need to have somebody to lead it. But who would that be? And what qualifications would he have?

I decided the assembly should have someone called a "pastor." I thought of this position as that of a shepherd; like a shepherd guiding his herd, the pastor in our assembly should be able to guide the believers on the right path. However, his main task would be to lead the assembly in prayer. It would also be his responsibility to conduct an annual festival honoring the patron saint for believers, as this was a visible and external aspect of the blessing of God. This would be both the pastor's duty and his right.

One of the main qualifications of the pastor would be an impeccable character. He also should have a leadership quality, so he might administer an assembly. It would also be his duty to protect his people from false prophets.

With Hose's help, I also began to decide on other necessary organizational matters. For example, when there are many assemblies in one region and thus more than one pastor, the pastors could elect someone to the position of what I called a "deacon." Besides having the basic qualifications of a pastor, the deacon should possess the ability to administer several assemblies simultaneously and have integrity and deep faith in God.

I appointed Hose as our first deacon. I had no doubt he was richly qualified for this post. Since he had more ability to understand and communicate in Greek than I, in the early days of our ministry, I had him talk to the natives about the kingdom of God and God's commandments. Fortunately, in due course, I proved able to converse with the natives easily, since I had read a few Greek classics in my younger days.

Hose and I occasionally exchanged ideas regarding the mission of our assembly and its organizational structure. Often I had thought about these matters and analyzed them for a long time on my own. However, the conversations with Hose were always illuminating for me, and I came to welcome them.

After the assembly for a particular week dispersed, Hose and I engaged in one such conversation. After thinking for a while, he asked me, "What is this assembly? Is it simply a gathering of people to talk about the kingdom of God?"

I responded with, "It's the congregation of people who are baptized by the Holy Ghost. We may even say it's their body. It's based on the services of the apostles."

"What is its mission?" Hose wondered.

"The assembly should always aim to work for the well-being of humanity. It should be an organic body that strives to bring justice and peace to the people. Let it be so! Now that our assembly is growing, what is your opinion about the procedures that we should follow in it?"

"Prayer should be the first ritual," Hose declared. "After that, confession; if one admits to sin, God will forgive him. Then Holy Communion, which will give people a sense of inclusion." Hose stopped for a while, immersed in thought. "How God's commandments are followed in heaven, so should they be on earth. People should pray for that. Those who forsake Jesus have no entry into the kingdom of God. This idea should be central to our message. We should also emphasize the importance of belief in the Holy Ghost."

I replied, "So our mission should be to make people aware of Jesus's teachings as they are and to assist them in following those in their lives. This will help them to attain salvation." I said this to assure Hose that I understood what he had said. "The believers in Syria and Egypt are following different rituals now. I do not think it's right. So we should prescribe common standards for them. Baptism also should be an important ritual."

Hose agreed with me on these points. After making arrangements for distributing clothes for poor folks the next day, I returned home.

With God's grace, our assembly grew in size, and I felt gratified. Gradually, I began to like my stay in Smyrna. New friendships brought hope. I sincerely believed I would be able to spread the message of Jesus in that land.

***

I would also like to record two events that occurred at this time that saddened me deeply. One was the death of Peter, the most important person among all the apostles. The other was the untimely death of Sabed, whom I regarded as my brother.

I came to know about the tragic death of Peter from a trader who was returning from Rome. The news of his passing pained me.

Peter was one of Jesus's earliest disciples and a staunch believer in his ideals. He revered Jesus very much. Although he had human weaknesses, he was in the forefront of spreading the message of the Lord. He was assassinated in the cruelest manner by a group of pagan worshippers who had the tacit support of Roman authorities.

It was said one assassin cut off Peter's head, thrust it on a spear, and exhibited it in the streets of Rome for the public to see. It was also rumored that many believers had been burned alive in Rome.

Fortunately, there were many who came to believe in Jesus.

Sabed's untimely death occurred two years after the start of our assembly in Smyrna. He had been traveling extensively, and at times he experienced difficulty obtaining hygienically prepared food in the different regions he went to. Eventually, his health began to deteriorate.

One day, while he was back in Smyrna, his body temperature rose very high, and he became unconscious. Thenorus sent a native physician to minister to him, but Hose and I were disappointed in his methods. We believed more in prayer.

On the fifth day, Sabed passed away peacefully to join our Father in heaven. His departure made a lasting wound on my heart.

CHAPTER 15

Sabed's passing made me concerned about Alka's future. Alka had been living with me since she was a child, and it had been many years since she had grown into adulthood. I was concerned that after I left the earthly world, there was no one left to look after her well-being. From time to time, I thought about it, and I started to make an attempt to find a suitable groom for her.

I found such a person in Sylvanis. From the moment I'd seen him in Magdala, I thought he was a man of integrity. He had been an enormous help in organizing our assembly in Smyrna. He was also sprightly—and handsome.

Sabed thought of Alka as his sister, and she in turn thought of Sabed as her brother. So I thought Sylvanis would be an ideal groom for her.

When I talked to Alka about my choice for her, she agreed to it. Under Hose's guidance, we decided to conduct her wedding to Sylvanis in Smyrna without an elaborate ceremony.

On the eve of the wedding, I hosted a banquet. I invited a few of my close associates, along with ten or twelve dignitaries of Smyrna who Thenorus had chosen. He had in his harem a number of beautiful women, and a few of them were adept at native dances. Their dancing added merriment to my banquet.

After the guests departed, I invited Aristha Hose for a discussion of time and space. During that time, I had begun to think about the return of Jesus. I was pondering questions about the meaning of one of his prophecies: *What exactly did he mean by his resurrection? Where is it going to happen? How long should we wait?* These were the concerns that prompted me to think about time and space.

I knew time and space do not have any form of their own—or any beginning or end. Space does not represent any quality of the objects by themselves. It's the form of all phenomena of the external senses. It's the subjective condition of our sensibilities, without which no external intuition is possible. As for time, it's nothing but the form of our internal senses—that is, our intuition regarding our internal state and ourselves. It's the formal condition of all phenomena.

Since in this universe, all objects—both movable and immovable—exist only in the emptiness of time and space, I believed that all that do not have a beginning or an end are one and the same. I surmised this oneness is the universe.

But who controls the events that take place in this universe? Is there even a supreme force like that? I wondered. I also wanted to know what the importance of mind was in this context.

Ultimately, I wished to know how I could discipline my mind to work for the welfare of Smyrna's oppressed people. Caring for others who are downtrodden is also at the core of Jesus's message.

I asked Hose, "Who controls the events in this universe? I have only a vague idea of what the universe itself is!"

He replied, "For that, we should decide what we mean by the term *universe*. To my knowledge, the universe is the combination of five elements."

"What are those five elements?"

"I have read a few books on this subject written by Greek scholars. I will tell you briefly what I learned from them."

"That will be very useful to me."

"The five elements are sky, fire, oxygen, water, and earth. Universe is the total sum of all these elements. We knew these elements through our external senses, by sight, touch, or smell. But we cannot understand time and space through our external senses. Since they cannot be understood by external senses, time and space do not have form, as you correctly think. But in the universe are activities such as creation, protection, and destruction."

"I understand," I said. "However, I would like you to explain it to me a bit more."

"We receive the knowledge about time and space—which are, in fact, internal and external intuitions—only through the five elements. The source of this knowledge is self. Mind is a medium through which the activities of the universe converge into the self. So it's through the senses that the mind gets knowledge about the universe. It follows, therefore, that the mind is essential to create awareness about time and space. So it's clear the working of humanity's mind is the decisive force controlling the activities in the universe."

I nodded. "So we must think about how to use our mind to uplift humanity! Look at the things that are happening around us: A poor peasant gives to the landlord his share of the crop, regardless of the annual yield. This pushes the peasant into perpetual poverty."

"Yes, it's so. The master should show him kindness."

"That's why the Holy Ghost is demanding landowners give to their vassals what they justly deserve."

"Yes, without creating any strife in society, we ought to uplift the poor through our ministry. That is the need of the present day."

***

I often sent Marcus to help Hose in his missionary work. He was a friendly young man who had become very instrumental in raising funds for our assembly. He was a convincing speaker too, a man full of energy.

I recall an incident that took place during one of our assembly's question-and-answer sessions. It shows, in those days, how cruely the landlords treated their tenets. His face was filled with fear and grief. He had difficulty even talking, so Marcus explained things to me in agonizing detail, as he had conducted an inquiry earlier to understand the privations the elderly peasant had gone through.

Apparently, the old man lived three or four miles away from our assembly, on a plot of land owned by a cruel and haughty landlord. The elderly man had a large family to support. Due to a lack of rain that year, he had experienced a very poor harvest and so could not give his landlord the appropriate share. The angry landlord had ordered the peasant's ears cut off as a form of punishment.

Only after considerable persuasion would the poor peasant sit down on a bench in front of me. He haltingly told me of the humiliation he still suffered at the hands of his landlord and that, most of the time, his family went hungry. His situation was heartbreaking indeed.

I prayed briefly and assured him that I would bring his situation before the area chief. I asked Marcus to give the peasant a monthly allowance from our assembly to mitigate his financial difficulties somewhat.

When Thenorus came to see me on some business matters, I told him of the plight of the poor peasant and that I wanted him to place the matter before the next village council meeting and recommend a suitable punishment for the landlord's cruelty. Thenorus promised he would do whatever I wanted him to do.

Through Marcus, I came to know that the elderly peasant's mistreatment wasn't an isolated incident. For example, I found out that in a small village in Smyrna, a landlord had used a yoke on two of his vassals and made them plow his plot of land, as his oxen were sick that day. The landlord wanted to complete the seeding before the next rainfall, and he had the vassals whipped if they were too slow in their work. Such news shattered me, and I went to bed early that night, after my evening prayer.

As I lay there, I felt an unusual numbness in my head. Then I heard hushed voices in the dark. I wondered, *Are the demons excised by Jesus trying to haunt me again?*

Not knowing what to do, but hoping to calm myself, I got up, read the Torah, and recited some hymns. Then I went back to bed and had a dream.

In a flower-bedecked boat, I reached a beautiful island. It had many fountains and golden trees. I could see deer running around merrily everywhere and swans happily swimming in nearby ponds.

In the center of that lovely island, I saw a glimmering palace studded with precious jewels. Inside that palace, in a beautifully decorated room, was the goddess of prosperity, piety, and generosity. She was the embodiment of beauty, grace, and charm.

She was seated on a lotus made of gold, the female energy of the supreme being that controls the activities in this universe. The kind goddess blessed me! First, in raising her right fingers up, she granted me refugee in her. Second, by bending back her left fingers, she granted me prosperity. The first sign denoted that she would protect her devotee from all dangers. With the second, she granted all that the devotee wished for.

I prostrated before the all-powerful goddess in thanks for her generosity.

The indulgent goddess blessed me and said, "You wanted to know in what way you can control your mind and use it as a tool to promote the welfare of humanity. There are many ways to do this. However, the most important way is to know me and worship me through the prescribed rituals. Since I am extremely pleased with you, all your wishes will come true. I am now giving you a part of my divine power."

The goddess gave me a brief smile and disappeared.

I bowed many times before the all-mighty goddess, the supreme energy that controls the universe.

When I woke up the next morning, I felt as if the vision I had in the dream had given me a new lease on life. This vision reminded me of the story of Goddess, at least the equal part of it. Here I'm referring to the story of the creation of earth. Also, in Judaism, God has never been viewed as exclusively male or female. In traditional Judaism, women are endowed with a great degree of intuition, understanding, and intelligence. I also knew that, in ancient times, our ancestors considered Miriam to be one of the liberators of the children of Israel, along with her brothers Moses and Aaron.

In ancient days, many imagined the deity as a female. This was acknowledgement of and respect for women as a source of life and fertility. In my mind, these thoughts were reinforced by the appearance of the female goddess seated on the golden lotus.

I wanted to apply the power derived from the concept of the Goddess: that people can change circumstances by the power within themselves.

I decided to embark on a quest for the inner meanings of hymns and rituals addressed to gods. After a lot of contemplation and reflection, I found that behind the many manifestations of God is the one who is the source of all, including God itself. This quest led me to acquire insight and knowledge of a kind that would set people free.

Daily I began to pray for the Goddess's blessings. After some time, I felt I achieved a measure of superior energy. I believed this came about through this deity's blessings.

I decided to use my newfound energy for the benefit of the people in

Smyrna and the surrounding areas. Since there were a large number of poor farmers who didn't own the land they cultivated, and their landlords often used repressive measures to extract their majority share of the farm produce, Marcus, Sylvanis, and I came up with a plan to address the issue.

First, we wanted to reduce the financial burden on the peasants. For example, in those years when the crop yield wasn't good due to a lack of rain, the peasants would not be required to give their landlords their full share. We wanted to reduce the shares by 40 percent during lean years.

A related demand was to end the practice of employing a peasant to a particular task without his consent. Third, capital provided by moneylenders should be made available to them at a reduced rate of interest, as part of the overall plan.

Having figured out a plan, we decided to educate and to organize the peasants so they would know about their rights and work toward achieving them.

We knew it was also important to bring these issues to the attention of village chiefs. After all, every human being needs to oppose injustice and greed. Sometimes doing so might require the use of force. Everybody should be prepared for that possibility, although the desire should always be to avoid such conflict if at all possible.

I also encouraged the pastors of several assemblies to issue statements supporting the rights of landless peasantry, while Marcus assembled a group of volunteers from among the peasants to coordinate these activities. He trained them for months.

One hundred peasants belonged to this group, and they ultimately called a meeting to articulate their demands. At that meeting, I addressed them with a short speech, making clear that I was willing to make any sacrifice on their behalf. I also assured them that the wrath of God would fall on landlords who exploited their vassals.

At that meeting, a delegation of twenty peasants—led by me—was formed to present our grievances and demands to each and every village chief. I also promised the peasants the complete cooperation of our assemblies in this effort.

Everyone present at the meeting listened to my speech with rapt attention. Afterward, the delegation members were a bit tense, probably because they were participating in activities with political undertones for the first time. However, we did manage to draft a resolution specifying our demands that we planned to give to the area chief, Thenorus, for his consideration. We wanted him to place this document before the area council at its next meeting and get it approved by that body.

I also advised the peasants not to go to work—even if their landlords demanded it—until their grievances were addressed.

After the meeting, we went to the residence of the village chief we had met when we landed on the beach after our arrival from Jerusalem. But as we approached the chief's house, nearly fifty peasants who were not part of the delegation joined us. I didn't know where they were from, and with a simple glance, it became evident that they would not hesitate to engage in violence. Some were carrying sickles they used in their work, while others had large sticks. And they were clearly agitated.

I decided to meet with the chief regardless. So I asked the assistant who was guarding his house to go and inform the chief of our arrival. The chief sent back word that he was ready to see Marcus, Sylvanis, and me. So in we went.

At that time, and without any provocation at all, three or four youths in the crowd started throwing stones at the chief's house. Though they didn't cause much damage, I was appalled. I came out of the house, admonished the stone throwers in sharp language, and asked them to leave the place immediately. They soon disappeared.

The village chief received us with kindness. He was annoyed at the stone throwing, and he promised to consider our demand before we left.

A few days after that event, Sylvanis told me something that made me exceedingly sad. Some of the landlords had spent huge sums of money and organized a group who, at the landlords' urgings, had burned down the houses of those who had accompanied me in the delegation.

I wouldn't let this incident stop me. I felt deeply the female goddess had given me unique talents with which I could change the world for the better. With renewed vigor, I showed my support for the peasants in their quest for justice.

I organized several rallies and meetings in which I condemned the landlords' inhumane actions. I even exhorted the peasants to face violence with violence. They were aroused by my words and actions, and they showed their willingness to endure any sacrifice for their cause.

The landlords became angry at this turn of events; never before had they faced such protests from their vassals. They were full of fear but also ready and willing to use any repressive measures necessary to subdue the peasantry. Tension prevailed everywhere.

Thenorus heard from his subordinates of all the developments that were taking place in Smyrna and the surrounding areas. In the beginning, he didn't regard them as serious. However, when he found out the peasants might stop working and that events were inexorably moving toward an open confrontation, he became very concerned. He sent me a message, asking for a meeting with me, and I agreed to see him.

Thenorus said to me, "I came over myself to tell you about a grave situation in my area. I learned from my staff that the peasants of Smyrna are going to stop their work in the fields. To combat this, their landlords are ready to face this rebellion with whatever methods they wish to use."

"What I heard is that violence has already been used by both parties," I said. "I know you will not justify the unjust and brutal activities of the landlords."

"What you say is right," he replied. "But is it not important to keep peace in the land? If the peasants stop working, our farm production will be nil, and this will invite many woes upon us. Even now, revenue to the national council has decreased by 60 percent. If the landlords embark on an open conflict, suppressing them will take considerable effort."

I sensed he was under considerable pressure from the landlords, so I asked, "What do you want me and my followers to do in this situation?"

He replied, "The peasantry will obey what you decree for the time being. Pacify them, and then stay away from our region for a while. Please do not misunderstand me. This is an earnest request. The landlords tell me that you are giving leadership to this movement. And the landlords have influence that they may use to undermine our financial stability. So if you accept my request, I will work toward getting their agreement on some of the issues that are important to the peasantry."

As I had dealt with Thenorus for years and knew him to be an honorable man, I told him he would have my reply in two or three days, after I thought through his request.

During those days, I prayed before the Goddess, the Supreme Power, to learn what she suggested in this matter. By then, I firmly believed that the Goddess, the source of all energy in the universe, is the guiding force that shapes the many activities in this universe. Ultimately, I realized and accepted that my relocation would help establish peace in Smyrna, my adopted home. It would also make Thenorus's task of getting the landlords to concede to at least some of the peasant's grievances easier. I knew that, over time, Thenorus would make matters right.

So I met with him again and told him I was agreeing to his request. Then, in consultation with him, I decided to move to a remote cave in the eastern mountains.[5]

***

The cave Thenorus selected for me was more than adequate for one person to live comfortably. Moreover, he constructed a fountain and a swimming pool inside the cave so I might indulge in water exercises. It was customary in those days to bring water into dwellings using aqueducts when the mountain snow melted in summer.

There was a table and chair inside the cave, so I could sit and write. Marcus even brought me a comfortable bed and cot.

I arranged with Thaddeus to have one meal a day prepared and asked that someone bring it over and place it on a stand in front of the main entry to the cave. I also thought of making a small garden in front of the cave but abandoned the idea later for reasons I don't remember.

***

As I spent time in the cave, I discovered I no longer wanted to see people in person. I devoted most of my time to worshipping the Goddess. As I remained unwed throughout my life, I felt there was nothing unusual in my becoming a devotee of female power at the last stage of my existence.

I began to wish that all the assemblies would come to worship female power. I didn't suggest any special ritual for this, but I sent word to Hose

---

[5] Archeologists from the United States and Israel have recently discovered many caves fit for human habitation in the mountains near the Mediterranean Sea. People have inhabited them since 300 BC. It's also believed that Israeli secret warriors who fought the Roman authorities often took refuge in these caves.

to install a statue of Mother Miriam in our assembly in Smyrna. I thought doing so might encourage Goddess worship.

Let me write that my obligation to Jesus remains priceless, as he was my teacher through much of my spiritual journey. I also want to thank everyone who helped me spread his message beyond the land of Israel.

***

To best worship the Goddess, I selected a unique and exhilarating posture. It required sitting on the floor with my legs straight. I then bent my right leg at the knee and held my right foot with my hands. Then I placed that foot at the root of my left thigh so that its heel was near my navel. Next I bent my left leg, and holding my left foot with my hands, placed it over my right thigh at the root, with its heel also near my navel. I made sure the soles of both my feet were turned up.

This position of crossed legs and an erect back kept my mind alert. It was also the pose most suitable for controlling my breathing. With this pose, my senses were turned inward, and rhythmic breathing calmed my mind's wandering, bringing a unique feeling of peace.

As I found clothing a barrier to sitting in this pose, I always discarded them first.

***

My mind has always craved new knowledge, but for a long time I had denied myself knowledge that comes through senses and through interaction with people. Now I see a number of small red-hot meteors coming straight toward me through the thick darkness in this cave.

Before they envelop my body, let me take my last breath.

CHAPTER 16

I, Alka, wish to write here my thoughts about my dear Mary, who was always like a sister to me.

For a very, very long time, Mary lived alone in a cave in an isolated mountain range. I do believe it will be useful to posterity to know my personal recollections surrounding the death and cremation of a savant who made an original contribution to the development of the early Christian church. Since I had the good fortune to observe, at close quarters, Mary's lifelong work on behalf of the dispossessed, I also think it's my duty to write.

***

It had been nearly twenty years since Sylvanis and I got married. After that event, I didn't really see Mary, for she was reluctant to mix with people during the last years of her life—even those who were dear to her. It was clear that she preferred to live like a hermit, away from the noisy world. She also instructed all of her loved ones to stay in Ephesus, since she thought we could do our missionary work more effectively there.

It was on a cold day, at sunset, that Mary's elderly cook, Thaddeus, came to the small house I shared with Sylvanis. His face was wrought with grief.

After resting for a while, he told us the reason for his visit. He had observed, for the last two or three days, that the food he placed carefully on the stand in front of Mary's cave wasn't touched. Fearing something was amiss, he informed Aristha Hose about it.

They both approached and entered the inner sanctum of the cave. Inside, they saw Mary's lifeless body on a mat made of bark. She was lying face up, as if in deep sleep. Her face was radiant.

Although Mary had spent many years in the cave, even during both the hot and cold seasons, her body didn't show any sign of decay. She was mostly naked, so they dressed her properly and carried her body to where Hose lived. Since he felt the rest of the details of what was to be done with Mary's body should be worked out in consultation with Sylvanis and me, he dispatched Thaddeus to us.

When I heard of the demise of Mary, whom I loved dearly like a sister, I fainted. Sylvanis attended to me tenderly. When I regained consciousness, we decided to travel to Smyrna the next morning.

When we reached Hose's house, he was waiting for us in the drawing room. After taking a shower, I went into the room where Mary lay, for a last look at her.

Although overwhelmed by extreme grief, I went near the body and kissed her on the forehead. I held both her hands in mine and stood there for a few seconds, as in a trance. Tears began to well up in my eyes.

My grandfather had given me to Mary to bring up when I was very young—indeed, a small girl! From that day on, I had participated in her moments of joy and tribulations. She treated me as her younger sister.

I cannot find words to write how I felt at her passing.

***

The first thing we did was cremate her body with honor and the appropriate rites. Since we thought, at that time, that we needed the blessings of the Lord our Savior, we prayed on our knees.

Our prayers were answered. We were able to find some flat land on the long road from Smyrna to Ephesus. It lay on the slope of a small hill on which there were shrubs with beautiful flowers. A few apple trees also graced the hill.

The congregation Hose started under Mary's guidance had grown in numbers over the years, and having heard of Mary's demise, around a hundred people from the assembly arrived for the cremation. In their presence and mine, the body of my sister was cremated.

As part of the ritual, the next day, Hose addressed the assembled believers with a short speech: "Mary was, indeed, a saintly woman who traveled and worked tirelessly with Jesus for many years to spread the gospel. May our Lord bless all who have come here to pay homage to our beloved sister. The best way to commemorate her memory is to believe in Jesus our Savior and to live our lives according to his teachings. Above all, Jesus taught us that we should love each other. Another follower of Jesus, the apostle John, has told you this several times.

"At this burial site, a sarcophagus will be built shortly in memory of Mary. In God's name, I ask you to make a pilgrimage to this holy place at least once a year and renew your pledge to live your life according to the Lord's teachings. May you all have his blessings."

***

For two days, Sylvanis and I stayed in Smyrna, giving instructions to Hose about what he needed to do from then on. Then we returned to our home in Ephesus.

Before returning to Ephesus and after consulting with the elders in Smyrna, I anointed Hose as the bishop of that assembly. He had worked tirelessly for many years and had earned the honor. The top shepherd in the assemblies in Rome and Greece was also known by this title, so we thought it appropriate to bestow this honor on Hose.

***

As everybody desired, in a few months, Hose built a sarcophagus at Mary's burial site and placed a large white marble cross on the spot.

I understand that even now many people are making annual visits to that hallowed place.

Printed in the United States
By Bookmasters